# GRANNY GOES ROGUE

## A SECRET AGENT GRANNY MYSTERY BOOK 8

### HARPER LIN

# ONE

When you're young, you never think about growing old. It's only when you reach middle age—say, forty or fifty—that reality sets in. Wrinkles appear. Your knees begin to hurt in damp weather. You get embarrassing and unprintable medical conditions. And as you pass through middle age and begin to approach retirement, you realize that aging is irreversible and it's your turn to go over that proverbial hill.

Well, sort of. If you've spent your entire youth (and a large part of your middle years) hunting down terrorists, toppling drug lords, and causing mayhem among every group of bad guys from Beirut to Bogotá, you don't really think about growing older. Aging is something that happens to other people. You're too relieved to make it through another day in one piece to worry about how each individual part is working.

Until you suddenly find yourself living with a cat in a cute little cottage in a sleepy bedroom district called Cheerville.

Then you know you're old, and I have to say it can be pretty darn annoying. Sure, I could still hit the bull's-eye at fifty yards with my 9mm automatic, but I had to wear my reading glasses to see the gunsights. I could still use a variety of martial arts to lay low a man half my age and twice my size, but I'd need several nights of hot baths before my joints and muscles stop screaming at me in protest.

It was a bit of a rip-off, if I must say. I'd been a specimen of physical perfection for nearly half a century until all those forced marches, battles, and jungle campsites began to catch up with me.

And now I had a bad case of lower back pain just when my family was about to celebrate my grandson's fourteenth birthday. I never used to get lower back pain. Joint pain from too many years firing guns and lifting heavy objects, sure. Occasional cricks in the neck from that time my head snapped back as my Kevlar helmet took a .303 round, oh yes indeed. But lower back pain? I didn't know where that came from. I couldn't recall ever being injured or straining my lower back.

That was frightening, because this new pain might be due to simple aging rather than my hyperactive lifestyle.

I'm Barbara Gold. Age: barely 71. Height: 5'5". Eyes: blue. Hair: gray. Weight: none of your business. Specialties: undercover surveillance, small arms, chemical weapons, Middle Eastern and Latin American politics. Current status: retired CIA agent, widow, and grandmother.

Addendum to current status: Fully aware of the fact that I was probably going to get the wrong gift for my grandson's fourteenth birthday because I was hopelessly out of touch with teen culture, and the one possible gift I had found had been crushed by a dead body landing in my shopping cart. I knew the man was dead because there was a large kitchen knife driven up to the hilt in the left ear, and the point was sticking out the right ear.

Perhaps I should back up.

I had been minding my own business, pushing a shopping cart around SerMart, a high-tech big-box store on the edge of town that sells everything from condiments to craft supplies in bulk. I'd already seen customers leave with thirty boxes of cereal and fifty pounds of toilet paper.

Huge shelves towered on either side of me as I walked down the jewelry section. Bracelets of every description were lined up on the shelves—from little silver friendship bracelets to hunky gold things that probably helped you work out your biceps and triceps merely by wearing them.

The bracelets came in boxes of four, six, ten, or twelve. The idea was that if you bought them in bulk, you would get a discount.

The shopping carts were equally oversized. I had taken the smallest-sized shopping cart available, and I had to practically do chin-ups to see over the top of the thing.

It wasn't helping with that back pain I mentioned, I can tell you.

So why was I in here, you might ask? I was asking myself the same question. Curiosity, more than anything else. I may be what many people consider old, but I try to keep up with the times. That can be useful, especially in my former line of work, and that training never goes away.

And SerMart certainly was part of the times. It had just opened to international press coverage because it was an experiment by the massive international online vendor Serengeti, which had become famous for its rapid delivery and cut-rate prices. Retail was something new for them, and I must say they still had some bugs to iron out.

Like not having any human beings anywhere in this labyrinth except at the cash registers.

They had talking drones instead, complete with facial and voice recognition software.

One floated down from the lofty reaches of the warehouse and hovered in front of me. I stopped.

"Hello," it said in a neutral female voice with not a trace of an accent. A little screen on the front showed a cartoon smiley face. "Are you having a good shopping experience?"

"Yes," I replied. Actually, I wasn't. I found this whole place depressing, but I was raised to have proper manners, even to flying robots.

"I noticed you have moved from the charms section to the bracelet section. Are you looking for something particular I can help you with?"

"It's for my grandson's birthday. He's going to turn fourteen this week, and he's having a bunch of his friends over. I thought it would be nice if they each got a present."

The cartoon smile widened. "Oh, how thoughtful! How old is your grandson going to be?"

Wow, the AI or whatever they call it in these things was pretty good. Or maybe they had someone in Calcutta listening in. On second thought, probably not. The English didn't have that strange lilting cadence the Indians bring to it. And the drone had missed a detail I had just mentioned.

"He's going to be fourteen," I repeated, speaking slowly. His birthday falls almost in the same week as mine, but we never celebrate with one single party for reasons that should be obvious. The teenage eye-rolling would be unbearable.

"Will there be girls coming to this party?" The monotone with which this was said made it sound odd. Couldn't the AI do a bit of *wink wink, nudge nudge?*

"Yes, boys and girls."

"That's great! We have some excellent jewelry packs for teen boys and girls. For example, there's our Sweetheart Pack, a charming—"

"Not the Sweetheart Pack," I interrupted the drone. "He'd be mortified."

"That's all right. We have plenty of great offers. There's the Street Kidz pack, the Young Artists Pack, the FriendZip Bracelet pack, the..."

I tuned out as the drone droned on. This was all a big mistake. I pushed my shopping cart around the hovering sales representative, which politely rose up to let me pass, then lowered down to my level again and followed at a respectful distance, still trying to sell me jewelry in bulk.

A package caught my eye. It was the FriendZip Bracelet Fun Pak. Why it would be spelled that way was not immediately apparent, but I did remember overhearing my grandson, Martin, talking about them with his friends. They were a New Thing.

New Things were good when you're fourteen. Old Things were not so good.

Old Things that provided New Things could be good though...

Yes, the opinion of a sloppy adolescent matters to me more than almost anything else in my life. I defy any one of you with a grandchild to say otherwise.

I picked up the package. It included a dozen FriendZip Bracelets. The idea, the blindingly colorful box explained in cool, hip lingo, was that you gave each of your BFFs one of the FriendZip Bracelets. It was a shiny cloth bracelet that unzipped on one side, and you could put FriendZip Tokens inside. These showed why your BFFs were your BFFs.

(Smug aside: "BFF" stands for "Best Friend Forever." Yes, I already knew that. No, I didn't have to look it up. I have a culturally superior grandson to explain these things to me, thank you very much.)

The FriendZip Bracelet Fun Pak came with a hundred ("Count 'em, *a hundred!*") FriendZip Tokens. These were colorful little metal thingies in the shapes of skateboards, footballs, video game controllers, hearts, etc. I supposed they would rattle inside the FriendZip Bracelet, so you could show off how many tokens you had and thus how popular you were.

Marketing genius.

A drone buzzed down to me and hovered over my shoulder. It winked at me. Actually winked.

"I see you have picked up the FriendZip Bracelet Fun Pak. What a great choice for the kid in your life! They are the latest fashion in all the middle schools and high schools."

The middle schools I could believe, but I couldn't imagine a sixteen-year-old wearing one of these. And all fourteen-year-olds aspire to be sixteen-year-olds. Would these be considered beneath them? Kids at this age are extremely picky, so picky I didn't know if in Martin's grade they were still a New Thing. They had been a New Thing a couple of weeks ago, but New Things can turn into Old Things before you know it.

Trust me, I know.

"Hmmm, I'm not sure," I murmured. "This may be passé already."

The smiley face was replaced with a flashing red exclamation mark. "Then all the more reason to act now! If you buy it in the next fifteen minutes, we'll take an additional ten percent off the retail price!"

"All right, but I get to take a selfie with you to show my grandson."

Was I trying too hard to be trendy? Yeah, probably. It's amazing how much grandparents crave approval of slouching, video game-obsessed grandchildren.

"I love selfies!" the drone said. The cartoon face was back, spinning around on the computer screen.

"Of course you do."

"Let's go to the checkout," it chirped. It actually sounded happy as it whizzed down the aisle and did a loop the loop.

I followed.

It was at this point that the body with the knife through its head fell into my shopping cart.

And right on top of my grandson's FriendZip Bracelet Fun Pak.

# TWO

I let out a horrific scream. I'm not generally prone to screaming, but the appearance of a dead body came as a shock, and I feel that since I've been a civilian for several years now, I can cut loose every now and then.

The drone buzzed back to me, the cartoon face surrounded by question marks.

"May I help you?"

"There's a dead body in my shopping cart!"

"I'm sorry, I don't understand."

"Do you think I do? A dead body just fell off the shelf and into my shopping cart!"

Then I got my head together and looked up, both to see if I could spot the murderer and check if there might be another dead body on its way down.

The shelves stood a good twenty feet tall. The lower ones had products for the customers to grab, while the upper ones held back stock. The tops of the shelves were connected by a series of catwalks with a steel mesh floor and railings on the sides. I would have been able to see anyone on the catwalks, but there was no one, just a few drones buzzing around, grabbing boxes for special air deliveries or to bring down to other clients.

Someone could be hiding on the top shelf, however. It was a good ten feet wide.

"Get me someone right away," I ordered the drone.

"I can help you with whatever you may need," it said pleasantly.

"No, a human being. I need an actual human being."

"Is there something the matter? Are you having a bad shopping experience?"

"Yes! I am having a bad shopping experience. Call security!"

"Security has been alerted by radio. What is the nature of the security issue?"

"There's a dead man in my shopping cart, what do you think?"

The drone buzzed over to the body.

"Sir, I must ask you to get out of the shopping cart. Shopping carts are for SerMart products only."

"He's dead, you idiot," I snapped, still scanning the top of the shelf. If the murderer or murderers were up there, they were still hiding. There was no way to get off that shelf except by taking the catwalk, and I saw no one. I just happened to be near a break in the shelves where another aisle crisscrossed mine, so stepping a few feet from the cart I could see the catwalk on the other side of the shelf too. No one had fled in that direction either.

"Where the heck is the murderer?" I said out loud.

"I'm sorry, I don't understand," the drone replied.

"I don't either."

I heard the sound of running feet. A middle-aged couple rounded the corner.

"What happened? We heard screaming. Argh!"

They ran back around the aisle.

"I presume that wasn't security," I said.

"Security will be here in just one moment."

Keeping an eye on the catwalks, I also checked out the body. He was thin, about six feet tall, with a fringe of gray hair around a bald pate. I guessed him to be about seventy, although he appeared to have been in good health before having a knife stuck through his head. It was one of those luxury knives with a keen steel blade that professional chefs use. Just the thing to drive through someone's head. It would take considerable strength, however.

More details: His clothes, while casual, were expensive. He wore shoes of soft Italian leather that must have cost several hundred dollars, and name-brand slacks and a dress shirt.

The most impressive part of his wardrobe was a heavy gold ring with a giant ruby framed with diamonds that he wore on the middle finger of his left hand. Generally, I find oversized jewelry to be tasteless, but this piece was so artistically crafted that it managed to be beautiful.

Assuming it was made with real gems and gold—and it sure looked like it was real—it must have been worth a pretty penny.

A simple gold wedding band was on the ring finger of the same hand.

After another glance at the catwalks, where the drones were still busily buzzing around on their various tasks, I approached the body for another look, and then immediately rushed back to the intersection of the aisles to see if the murderer took the opportunity to make a break for it. No luck.

"Are you lost?" the drone said. "Can I help you find anything in particular?"

"How about security?"

"Security will be here in just one moment."

"You've mentioned that before."

I went and took a closer look at the body. The knuckles on the right hand were scuffed. There was very little blood on the entry or exit wound, but I could see faint traces where blood had been cleaned incompletely off the skin on the head and neck. A few fresh drops dripped out of the wound, staining the victim's otherwise clean shirt. No doubt the fall had shaken the head and released some blood that remained in the body.

I touched the flesh of his hand. It was cold but not completely cold. A body will reach the surrounding temperature, and thus feel cold to the touch since we're used to bodies being warm, within about twenty hours. Either this man had been killed within that time frame or he had been kept in a warm place. I didn't see any other signs of decomposition.

I flexed the arm. It was stiff but not completely so. Rigor mortis starts around four to six hours after death. I suspected that this man had been killed, cleaned, redressed, and most likely moved here about eight hours before he made his uninvited entry into my shopping cart.

I checked my watch. Just past eleven. So whoever killed him did it in the wee hours of that morning.

But why move him here? He didn't seem like the kind of person to be hanging around a big-box store at three o'clock in the morning.

As I pondered all this, I heard a strange sound. It sounded for all the world like an old steam train. *Puff puff puff puff. Puff puff puff puff.*

I looked around for tracks. Yes, really. I wouldn't put anything past this weird place.

The puffing got louder and began to be accompanied by a rhythmic thudding.

A security guard came huffing and puffing around the corner, sweat pouring down his face. His brown polyester shirt had popped out of his matching pants to show a large white belly with a fringe of hair around the belly button. I looked away, only to spot the dark stains under his armpits. I looked at the corpse instead. It was more pleasing to the eye.

"Oh my God!" the security guard moaned. "He's dead."

"Dead as a doornail," I replied. "Dead as Caesar."

The security guard looked at me, eyes wide. "There's another man dead?"

"I don't know. Is there?" I asked, confused.

"Caesar. Who's this Caesar? You said he was dead too."

"Oh, Lord. It's just a saying. He died well before your time. Even before my time."

The guard looked at the body in my shopping cart. A drone buzzed above him, looking too.

"Sir," the drone said. "I must ask you to get out of the shopping cart. Shopping carts are for SerMart products only."

The security guard frowned at the drone. "Go away. Security override."

"Have a nice day," the drone said, buzzing away.

"God, I hate those things," he said, looking back at the body.

"You and me both."

"When I heard the security call, I was in the office. I looked at the camera and saw this guy in your cart and thought he was drunk. That happens sometimes."

"He might have been drunk, but that knife in his

head makes me think he's got more problems than overindulgence in alcohol."

"What happened?"

"I was hoping you could tell me. I was walking along, and this body fell into my shopping cart. It fell from up there somewhere. I've been watching, but I haven't seen anyone up there."

"We keep it locked during store hours to keep kids from getting up there and spitting on the customers."

"How very thoughtful of you."

"The door to get up there is only open after hours so the night shift can move stuff around."

"You might want to check that the door is still locked."

The security guard nodded. "Yeah." He unclipped a walkie-talkie from his belt and plugged in an earphone so I couldn't hear. I felt rather left out. The body was in my shopping cart, after all. "Mary? Call the police. We have a dead man in aisle six. Yeah, a dead man. No, really dead. And check the door to the service stairs. Make sure it's locked. But don't touch the knob, all right? The cops will want to dust for fingerprints." There was a pause as a voice crackled in his earphone. "No, I'm serious. Someone really is dead, not like last time."

He got off the walkie-talkie.

"Not like last time?" I asked.

"Last week there was a zombie flash mob."

"A zombie flash mob?"

"They organize it on social media. A bunch of people show up at a store acting like regular customers, then one of them pretends to have a heart attack. Another one plays the doctor, who comes over to help and declares the man dead. Then the guy pretending to be dead gets up and starts attacking all the onlookers. He bites them and they turn into zombies. Scared the hell out of me. We had zombies everywhere."

"Was this some sort of protest?"

Serengeti.com was an innovative company and a controversial one. Maybe they were inspiring equally innovative protests.

"No, they just do it for fun."

I had nothing to say to that. Some of the things people get up to these days really make me feel out of touch.

Although that's not necessarily a bad thing.

The security guard's radio crackled.

"What's that? The door's locked? Okay, thanks, Mary. Go through the store and keep an eye on the catwalks."

There was another crackle on his earphones.

He turned to me. "The police are on their way. My colleague just called them."

"And the door upstairs is locked?"

"Yes, there's no other way up there. You say the body just fell?"

"That's right."

He looked up at the shelves, scanning the upper reaches of the giant warehouse for a murderer who was apparently not there. He wiped the sweat from his brow and scratched his head. He was still out of breath from his marathon run across the store.

"This doesn't make any sense," he murmured.

"No," I replied. "This doesn't make any sense at all."

# THREE

The worst part about uncovering a murder in this sleepy little suburb is that I have to deal with Police Chief Arnold Grimal.

In Police Chief Arnold Grimal's opinion, the worst part about uncovering a murder in Cheerville is that he has to deal with me.

Murders seem to congregate around me. I hadn't been here an entire season before a member of my reading group got bumped off. This was followed by a rapid succession of murders that almost included the world's most famous movie star. I had come to Cheerville to retire from a life of danger, and my life of danger figured it was too young to kick up its feet and decided to continue its career.

Arnold Grimal did not look like a symbol of

authority. He was a lifelong desk jockey who, until my ill-starred appearance, mostly dealt with parking offenses and cats stuck in trees. He wore a cheap yellow suit that did not hide the sweet-and-sour sauce stains from his favorite Chinese takeaway restaurant. He slouched into SerMart (he has worse posture than my teenaged grandson), and his face fell when he saw me.

"Why am I not surprised?" He groaned.

"Nice to see you too."

He had taken a good twenty minutes to respond to a 911 call about a dead body. By this time, SerMart's two security guards had cleared the store of all the customers. Now a cluster of employees stood by the cash registers, herded there by a nervous-looking woman in a gray business dress who I took to be the manager.

"So, what happened?" Grimal asked the security guard who was standing beside me. The fellow had finally caught his breath but was still sweating, I suppose more from stress than exertion. He was a bit odoriferous, I must say.

"A dead body fell in her shopping cart," said the security guard, whose name, I had finally learned, was Bob.

Grimal slumped a little more. "Of course it did."

He turned to a pair of policemen who had just come up.

"Search the building. Lock all the doors. Make sure no one gets in or out."

"I'll help you," said a second security guard, who I took to be Mary.

The woman in the gray suit clacked up in high heels.

"I'm Florence Nightingale."

"And I'm Sherlock Holmes," Grimal replied.

I burst out laughing. The cashiers all took a step back. You shouldn't laugh at a murder scene. "It's not a good look," as my son says.

The manager frowned. "Florence Nightingale is my real name. My parents wanted me to be a nurse."

"And instead you ended up managing SerMart," Grimal said.

"Is there something wrong with that?" she snapped.

Grimal shrugged. "Not as long as you stick to one murder per year. You have to get a permit for more."

I cocked an eyebrow. Was Grimal developing a sense of humor? Maybe he was hanging around me too much.

"Let's go look at the murder scene," she huffed

and clacked away. Grimal, Bob the security guard, and I all followed.

The poor murder victim (actually, rich murder victim) was lying in my shopping cart, his arms and legs draped over the side, just where we had left him. A drone hovered nearby, telling him to get out.

"Go away!" snapped Florence Nightingale, waving her hands like she was shooing a fly. "God, I hate those things."

The drone buzzed off.

Grimal looked at the body. "Oh no, it's Sir Edmund Montalbion!"

"And who is Sir Edmund Montalbion?" I asked.

"He is the richest man in Cheerville," Florence Nightingale said, going pale.

"Was," I corrected.

"Was," Grimal nodded sadly.

"You know him?" I asked the police chief.

"Not very well. He was a regular contributor to various charities. Once he asked for police advice about making his home burglarproof. He installed the best security equipment money could buy, along with safes good enough for a bank and an excellent CCTV system linked directly to the region's biggest security company. Monitored twenty-four seven. We assured him that with that level of protection, no one would rob him."

"What did he need to protect?"

"Sir Edmund Montalbion collected gemstones like some people collect stamps."

"Did he have any stamps in the house?" I asked.

Grimal's brow furrowed in confusion, a common expression with him. "I suppose he had one or two."

"So he collected stamps like some people collect gemstones."

"Let's just deal with this case, all right?"

I grinned. Grimal's training was coming along nicely. He had already resigned himself to the fact that I'd be helping with the case.

I turned to the manager. "Did you know him?"

"I've met him several times at gem shows and auctions. He never talked to me much, though. He didn't like the idea of SerMart."

"Too commercial and corporate for his taste?"

She frowned. "Something like that."

"Odd he would end up here, then," I mused.

"I can't believe this is happening," Florence Nightingale huffed. "Our quarterly assessment is next week."

"Did he have any association with the store? Was he ever a customer?" Grimal asked.

Florence Nightingale shook her head. "No. He generally bought at auctions or privately. He was a big name in the jewelry business. A bit of a snob, to be honest. He wouldn't be caught dead in a store like... oh."

The manager covered her mouth and turned a brilliant shade of scarlet.

Grimal started taking photographs of the crime scene. Cheerville was too small a town to afford a dedicated police photographer, so he did the job. At least he was a better photographer than detective. Dead bodies don't try to outwit you.

After he finished, he dusted for prints on the shopping cart and the victim's two rings, felt the man's flesh, and experimented with bending his limbs.

"Been dead several hours but not much more than that," he muttered. "His flesh is almost room temperature and rigor mortis is just beginning."

Congratulations, Grimal, you passed the final exam for Dead Bodies 101.

He rifled through his pockets.

"Nothing."

"A man doesn't generally go out in the early hours of the morning without his car keys and wallet," I said.

"They could have been taken from him," Grimal said in a superior tone. "A panicked attempt to hide his identity. Plus, he probably carried a fat wad of cash that would be a temptation for the murderer."

"Oh dear, Grimal, I gave you a chance to one-up me and you missed it. When I said he should have had his keys and wallet, you should have pointed out his clothes had been changed."

Grimal blinked. "His clothes have been changed?"

I gestured at the clothes. "Almost no bloodstains. What there is on them came when the head wound got jarred by his meteoric entrance into my shopping cart. And notice that his face has been washed, probably in haste or under low-light conditions. You can still see a few traces of bloodstains. When the coroner strips him, he'll probably find the same with the rest of the body. A wound like that would have left his clothes and body soaked with blood."

"Well, of course," Grimal blustered.

Florence Nightingale looked from me to Grimal and back again. "Which one of you is the police officer?"

"I am," we said in unison.

"Well, whichever of you is, could you please clean up this crime scene so we can reopen? I have a quarterly sales target to reach, and they're checking next week!"

"But you only opened two weeks ago," I said.

She glared at me like I had said the stupidest thing in the world. "Serengeti.com has *quarterly* quarterly sales targets and assessments. That means every three weeks."

"That's stupid," Grimal said. Harsh words, coming from someone like him.

Florence Nightingale turned her glare on him. "It's innovative and cutting-edge. Everything Serengeti.com and its associated companies do is innovative and cutting-edge."

"Such as having dead bodies fall into customers' shopping carts," I said. "I've never had that retail experience before."

Florence Nightingale let out a shriek. Grimal struggled with the holster beneath his jacket and finally managed to draw his gun, looking around for the murderer. The sight of the gun made Florence Nightingale shriek again.

"Why are you waving your gun around?" she shouted.

"Because you're screaming, I thought..."

"I'm screaming because I didn't realize she was a customer," she rounded on Bob the security guard. "Why didn't you tell me she was a customer?"

Bob shrugged.

"Ohmygodohmygodohmygod. Please don't sue. Oh, *please* don't sue."

I patted her on the shoulder. "Calm down. I won't sue."

"We'll give you a gift voucher," she said, brightening up like she just had a stroke of genius. "Yes, a hundred... no, a *thousand*-dollar gift voucher. I'll take it out of my personal savings. Just don't tell anyone you're a customer. There's a quarterly quarterly assessment coming up. My God, if the regional manager finds out..."

"I promise not to tell. The gift voucher isn't necessary."

She got a look of profound shock on her face. "Yes, it is! If a customer suffers extreme stress or shopping dissatisfaction in our store and we don't offer a gift voucher from our personal savings, Serengeti.com can sue us. It says so in the contract!"

"All right. Make it out for a dollar."

She paused. Considered. "You know? That might just work."

"Could we all focus on the dead body, please?" Bob the security guard suggested.

We all looked at each other, abashed.

Grimal got back to work, taking some more photos and then asking Bob to take us up to the catwalk. He led us to the rear of the store, through an employee break room and office, and to another door. It stood open with one of the policemen standing guard.

"We checked upstairs, sir. There's no one. My partner and the other security guard are checking the grounds."

"Did you dust for fingerprints?" Grimal asked.

"Yes, sir. Got a bunch, sir, as one would expect from a commonly used door."

"That's going to be a pain for the lab," Grimal mused. He turned to Florence Nightingale. "We'll need to get fingerprints from every one of your employees."

"We have those on file."

Grimal cocked his head. "You fingerprint all your employees?"

"Reduces the chance of workplace theft."

"But not murder," I said.

Grimal turned to the officer. "You stay here. We're going up."

We ascended a long flight of concrete steps, Bob huffing and puffing, me huffing and puffing almost as much, Florence Nightingale cursing and having to take off her heels, and Grimal grumbling. I couldn't make out the words. Then I realized it wasn't his voice grumbling but his stomach. It was about time for lunch. Those sweet-and-sour sauce stains must have been from yesterday's lunch.

The stairway opened up onto a small landing of steel mesh and a labyrinth of catwalks spreading out every which way. It was open to the store below, and we could see dozens of aisles of shelves piled high with goods, drones flying above and along them.

"This place is huge," Grimal said.

"The largest retail store in the state," Florence Nightingale said proudly.

"What are the chances that the body would fall right into my shopping cart?" I said.

"Pretty close to zero," Grimal said. "You think someone is targeting you?"

"Now who would target little old me?" I said in as innocent a voice as possible. I tried to keep the irony out of my tone. Really, I did.

"I can think of a million people," he grumbled. "Let's work through this place systematically and make sure no one is up here."

It didn't take as much time as the size of the store would suggest. The catwalks were all clearly visible to one another so as soon as we got away from the landing we could see the entire network. No one was up on this level. There was nowhere to hide and no back way to escape through.

I pointed to an area of the catwalk.

"The body fell from somewhere over there."

We headed that direction until I could see my shopping cart down below, the body of poor old Sir Edmund Montalbion lying slumped inside, a drone hovering next to him. From far below, we heard its tinny voice say, "Sir, I must ask you to get out of the shopping cart. Shopping carts are for SerMart products only."

We got right above the spot. The light was rather dim, the main fluorescent lamps that illuminated the shop floor hanging below the catwalk. We only got the reflected light. I suppose this was to make the work area less visible to the shoppers. Indeed, I hadn't noticed it in my peripheral vision until I had looked up to see where the body had dropped from.

Grimal pulled a Maglite out of his pocket and flicked it on, shining it all along the catwalk. There was nothing there. I didn't see any traces of blood. We peered closer.

"Look at that," Grimal said, pointing.

There were several scrapes along the railing at

the spot from which the victim had fallen. The metal was shiny, like it had been scraped with another metallic object.

"You see lots of scrapes like that up here," Bob the security guard said. "The night crew is always carrying loads around. Makes a big racket when they bang against the railings."

"Do you know which employees were doing this?" Florence Nightingale asked him. "They should get a written warning."

Bob paled. "I, um, I didn't see, ma'am."

"These look fresh," I said, bending close to the marks. My back twinged in protest.

"They're always moving heavy objects over the side," Bob said with a shrug.

"How do you get them down to the shelves?" I asked. The middle shelves were a long way down.

"We have ladders with adjustable platforms that you can make go up and down with an electric motor," Florence Nightingale said. "We have crews working up here and down at the shop floor. But they only move the boxes that weigh more than 30 pounds. The lighter boxes are lifted by drone. That makes everything move quicker. It's an innovative and cutting-edge method of stocking the shelves."

"Everything Serengeti.com and its associated

companies do is innovative and cutting-edge," I said before she could.

"That's right," Florence Nightingale and Bob the security guard said, their heads nodding in unison.

I got right above my cart. There were several scrapes on the railing for a patch of about five or six feet. They did, indeed, look quite fresh. I moved along the catwalk for a time. Bob was right, there were scrapes all along the railing. Some fresh, some not. But that cluster of fresh scrapes right above the body made me wonder.

I peered down again and noticed something.

"What's that?" I asked, pointing. A white bit of paper was stuck to one of the metal struts holding up the bottom of the catwalk right beneath my feet.

## FOUR

"I don't see anything," Grimal said, leaning out and trying to look where I was pointing.

"That's because your belly keeps you from leaning out far enough," I said.

"Hey, that's fat shaming," the police chief objected.

"Do be quiet."

Florence Nightingale leaned out, her thin frame bending over the railing.

"Oh, that's a label," the manager said.

She lay down on the catwalk and reached down. She had to stretch to reach, with Grimal hovering in the background with his arms out, worried she might slip over the edge but too shy to actually grab hold of her. Considering how high-strung she was, that was probably wise.

She peeled it off, stood, and held it out to Grimal. It was a small label about the size of two postage stamps set side to side with a bar code on it. The back was sticky. Sticky enough, in fact, that she had some trouble getting it off her finger. Before I could say anything, she had mangled the thing, smearing her fingers all over it and obscuring any fingerprints that had been on it previously.

Grimal put it in a plastic evidence bag, but I doubted he'd learn anything from it now.

"It probably just fell off a package," she said.

"Yeah, probably," Grimal agreed, "but we have to look at all angles."

We looked around and found nothing more of note, except for a few drones floating around with small boxes clutched in their set of four little mechanical pincers on the bottom of their bodies.

Bob then showed us a freight elevator that led to the loading dock. It was turned off at the moment, the main switch secured behind a locked electrical panel. Only management had the key. The loading dock was also locked and empty.

"Let's go back to the office and scan that bar

code," I suggested. "Then we can watch the security video."

"All right," Florence Nightingale huffed. "But let's make it quick. We need to reopen."

"We need to check the crime scene for any significant details and then take the victim out before that can happen," Grimal said.

"Indeed," I agreed. Grimal looked askance at me.

At the back room we'd passed through previously, Bob grabbed a scanner and checked the bar code. It was for a ten-pack of gold bracelets, because doesn't everybody want to buy their gold bracelets in quantities of ten? The retail price was $199.99, so I had to wonder how much gold was actually in these gold bracelets.

That was neither here nor there. It wasn't a very expensive item compared to some of the other bulk jewelry boxes I'd seen in that aisle, so it wasn't something that was likely to have been stolen. Perhaps it really had fallen off a box.

We checked in the aisle. Out of the twenty boxes of gold bracelets, all of them had their bar-code stickers.

"Must have been stolen by one of the night shifts," Grimal said.

"They get searched on their way out," Bob said.

"Searched?" I asked.

The manager nodded. "Oh yes. We have male and female security guards on staff during every shift. That way we can strip-search everyone."

My jaw dropped. "I've never heard of someone having to get strip-searched while working a retail job."

Florence Nightingale gave me a haughty look.

"The employees like it. If they get strip-searched, there's no suspicion of theft. That way the employees can go about their duties with a clean conscience, knowing they won't get falsely accused, like what happens at so many other retail outlets."

I glanced at Bob to see what he thought of this ridiculous statement, but he was staring into space, as if imagining himself somewhere far, far away.

"How about we go look at the security camera footage?" Grimal said.

We tromped over to the security office, which was clear on the other side of the store. As we passed the cash registers, Florence Nightingale frowned at the cashiers standing huddled, wide-eyed under the watchful gaze of one of Cheerville's finest.

"Why aren't you working?" she demanded.

They looked at each other and back at her.

Florence Nightingale tapped her foot, hands

balled into fists on her hips. "Well?"

"There are no customers," one ventured.

The manager waved her arm dramatically at the shelves. "Then work on stock! Clean up the shelving. Make sure the boxes are straight. What is the motto?"

"There's always something to do at SerMart," they intoned. "Idle hands pull down profits."

I exchanged glances with Grimal. He looked equally appalled.

The police chief cleared his throat. "Just avoid aisle six. That's where the body is. And no one goes upstairs to the catwalks. You"—he pointed to a police officer—"stand guard at the murder scene."

"Yes, sir," the policeman said, moving away. The employees moved away too. There wasn't a straight back in the entire crowd.

The security office was a high-tech affair, what the employees of Serengeti.com would call "innovative and cutting-edge." A large bank of computer screens showed various points in the store. Unlike most security cameras, these were high quality, with crystal-clear images. I've never understood why people feel safe with bargain-basement cameras that give such grainy images you can't recognize anyone on them. I've actually seen defendants go free because even though they were caught on camera, the picture quality was so poor that their lawyers were able to make convincing cases that it wasn't them.

Not so with these cameras. As they tracked the employees going about their tasks, I could recognize every feature. I could practically read the lips of the ones speaking to each other.

As Bob fiddled with the computer files to find the moment when the body made its unwelcomed entry into my shopping cart, I looked around the rest of the office. There was a male and a female "changing room"—a pleasant euphemism for being forced to take your clothes off in front of a coworker —a line of walkie-talkies on a shelf, and a state-of-the-art burglary alarm. I noted the make and model.

"Here we go," Bob said. I turned... and was treated to an image of myself talking to a drone.

"You two seem to be getting along," Grimal said with a chuckle. "Is there sound on this thing?"

"The state wouldn't let us rig the store with mics. Something about the right to privacy," Florence Nightingale said. She almost sounded disappointed.

Just at that moment, the body of Sir Edmund Montalbion plunged into the cart.

Seeing myself from a remove, I could tell I did

not react well. I jumped back, hands waving in the air, my mouth forming an O as I let out a silent scream. I spun around, screaming in all directions, my hands still waving in the air. I hadn't remembered that part.

Grimal snickered. "Now that's what I call an innovative and cutting-edge shopping experience." I shot him a nasty look. He pointed to the knife through the victim's head. "Get it? Cutting-edge?"

Bob and Florence Nightingale stared at him.

"Can I see some identification?" Bob asked.

Grimal's brow furrowed. "What for?"

"To make sure you're really chief of police."

"Oh, he is," I said as Grimal sputtered. "And this is actually him on a good day."

"How about we review the tape and find the suspect?" the police chief grumbled.

We rewound the tape, following me backwards through my long and fruitless search for my grandson's birthday gift. We could not see anyone tailing me or taking any interest in me. We then shifted to other customers, tracing them as they went through the store. We saw nothing suspicious.

"Okay, let's switch to the catwalk," Grimal said.

"We don't have cameras up there," Florence Nightingale said.

"Why not?" I asked.

"To save money, mostly. These cameras are expensive, and it costs a lot of employee hours to keep track of them all. There are no customers up there to monitor, and with all the employees being strip-searched at the ends of their shifts, there really is no need."

"Wonderful," Grimal moaned. "You have cameras watching every spot *except* the murder scene?"

Florence Nightingale shrugged. "Sorry."

"Wait," I said, pointing to a camera on the ceiling. "The security office is filmed too? Why don't I see that on the monitors?"

"The security office is monitored from the manager's office," Bob said, his voice flat.

"Is there a security camera in the manager's office?" Grimal asked.

"Yes. That's monitored from the Regional Manager's office."

*I need to get out of here,* I thought.

"Fine," Grimal said with a sigh. "Switch to the camera covering the doorway leading upstairs and rewind over the past several hours. The victim died in the early hours of this morning, so he must have been killed here or moved here around that time."

Bob did as he was asked. We watched in fast reverse as the doorway stood unused through the morning until an hour before opening time, when we suddenly started to see employees going in and out. We watched them closely, looking for anyone who wasn't in an employee uniform or anyone who was carrying a bag or box big enough to contain the late Sir Edmund Montalbion.

Nothing.

Stumped, we reviewed the previous day and night, spending more than two hours staring at people moving jerkily backwards at high speed. It was wearing on the eyes, I can tell you. Still nothing.

We then went back to the night when the victim was murdered and went through more slowly, freeze-framing on every face, hoping to spot someone who was wearing an employee uniform but wasn't actually employed at SerMart. Bob and Florence Nightingale were able to identify every one of them.

"Is there any way to get into the upstairs gallery from the roof?" Grimal asked. I raised an eyebrow. He was being unusually thorough today.

"There is an emergency exit up there, but the alarm sounds if it's opened. There's no record of an alarm. Besides, it's locked from the outside. You can go out but not in."

"Do you have cameras covering the outside?"

"Yes, but not the roof. We'd be able to see anyone climbing up, though."

We ran through the past forty-eight hours. Nothing.

"We're getting nowhere," Grimal grumbled.

"Surely you must be used to that by now," I said with my sweetest sweet-little-old-lady smile.

Before he could say anything, a red warning light flashed on one of the camera feeds and a little buzzer sounded.

"What's that?" we both asked.

Bob pointed. One of the employees, an older man with a potbelly that put Grimal's to shame, was leaning against a shelf, mopping his brow.

"He looks worn out, the poor dear," I said. "Is that some sort of medical alarm?"

Florence Nightingale shook her head. "The cameras are programmed to spot any lack of movement among the employees. We then sight check them to see what they're doing. If they're not working at the assigned pace, they lose Productivity Points. A low Productivity Point score can keep them from being promoted or getting a raise. And, oh dear..."

She was watching a computer spreadsheet Bob

had opened up. He had run down a list of employees to a name, Preston La Salle. I could see the name on the sick employee's name tag. Bob went through several columns of data to one marked Productivity Points. He lowered the points from eighty-five to eighty.

"I knew he'd fail," Florence Nightingale said. "Wonderful. Another awkward conversation for this shift."

"What do you mean?" I asked.

"The Productivity Points are scaled to maximize productivity. If they fall below a certain point, the employee is terminated and we hire someone else. We have a lot of applicants, so that's not a problem."

I made an angry gesture at the man still trying to catch his breath. "But he looks ill!"

"All the more reason to let him go. Health insurance payments will cut into our profit margin, and I will lose some of my own Productivity Points."

I treated her to a level gaze. She took a step back, shocked. I can have a nasty glare when I want to.

"If you tell me that practice is innovative and cutting-edge," I said in a low voice, "there are going to be two murders in your shop today."

"Okay, okay!" Grimal cried, raising his hands while the two SerMart employees went pale. "It's been a stressful day for all of us. How about we all calm down, shall we?"

"I'm quite calm," I said, keeping my voice soft and even. I've found that people are far more intimidated by someone who doesn't lose their cool than someone who does. It helped when I had an M-16 in my hands, but in our overly litigious society, you don't need one.

Grimal turned to the manager. "Have you fired anyone recently?"

"We've only been open two weeks," Florence Nightingale said.

"You didn't answer my question."

"We've only fired five people so far."

"Only?" Grimal and I said in unison. We glanced at each other. We kept replying in an identical manner. We really needed to stop doing that.

The manager shrugged. "If they dip beneath the minimum acceptable Productivity Point level, it's out of my hands."

"Have any of these former employees made threats against the company or tried to come back onto the premises?"

"No."

Grimal sighed and scratched his balding head. "Well, give me a list of them anyway. I'll also need a list of everyone who has access to the building's keys and security codes."

"I'll get those for you," Florence Nightingale said. She looked at the camera, where several men and women in white forensic crime-scene-examiner suits were studying the dead body in my shopping cart. "Oh! Your CSI team is here. Could they please get this done as soon as possible?"

"Yes, you wouldn't want a human tragedy to affect sales," I quipped. "that might lower your Productivity Point level."

The manager failed to take the bait. Instead she looked worried.

"It would," she whispered. "Oh yes, it would."

I spent another dreary two hours in the store making a statement and looking over the shoulder of the CSI team before I could go. The fluorescent lights and canned music had given me a piercing headache.

As I made my retreat toward the parking lot, Florence Nightingale stopped me at the door. She held out a gift-wrapped package with an envelope on top.

"A peace offering," she said with a forced smile. "We got off on the wrong foot, and I don't want you to think ill of me. I'm not a bad person. I'm only doing my job."

*How many times have I heard that one?* I thought.

"What is this?" I said, taking the package.

"A FriendZip Bracelet Fun Pak to give your grandson. I hope he has a great birthday. The envelope has that gift certificate I mentioned."

I was about to say something cutting until manners took over. She was required to give the gift certificate, and was kind enough to give the FriendZip Bracelet Fun Pak too. This woman must have realized how ridiculous the rules at her place of employment were, but she was just a cog in the wheel.

A wheel that must breed a lot of resentment. I wondered if that resentment had led to murder.

But why the murder of someone who wasn't even associated with the business?

I had a lot of questions to answer about this case and far too few leads.

In the meantime, however, I had a greater challenge to face.

I had to be cool around an almost fourteen-year-old.

# FIVE

After the retail purgatory of SerMart, the chaos and noise of my grandson's bedroom was a positive relief.

I found him lying out on his bed, texting his friends. The radio was tuned to KRAP, the local hip-hop station. The loud boasts about "slinging ice" and "capping homies" made for weird background music in a room that still showed evidence of a little boy in residence.

Martin had not entirely given up his teddy bears, for example. Granted, they were tucked in one corner of a shelf, but the mere fact that they were in a tidy row on the shelf when most of his belongings were lost in the landfill on the floor spoke volumes. My daughter-in-law, Alicia, had told me that sometimes she'd peek in on him at night to make sure he was all right and find those bears in bed with him. That happened especially when there was a thunderstorm outside or if she and my son, Frederick, had one of their rare fights.

It's what I found so charming about boys and girls Martin's age, that mixture of bravado and vulnerability. Their pose of independence and their sneaking ways of looking for support and reassurance.

"Grandma!" he shouted, vaulting off his bed by pumping his legs up in the air, slamming them down on the mattress, and thus propelling himself into a standing position. I wistfully remembered a time when I was that limber. "You finished the book yet?"

"Yes, I have," I replied, pulling out a copy of *Cargo Blasters #3: Mars Marathon Manglers* from my purse. It was the latest young adult series we were reading together. It was about a bunch of teenaged space truckers fighting aliens and interstellar pirates. It had all the elements a nearly fourteen-year-old boy would want—large machines, laser battles, zero gravity skateboarding, and just the barest hint of flirtation between the main male and female characters.

To be honest, I found it formulaic and

predictable, but then I'd been reading for a good five decades longer than he had. Besides, I wasn't going to pass up the opportunity to bond with my grandson. He loved reading, although he was finicky about what he read, and he didn't have another adult showing interest. My son wasn't much of a reader, and my daughter-in-law mostly read advanced physics journals.

"I'll give you number 4, *Passage to Pluto*. Don't you think it's unfair that Pluto is only a dwarf planet?"

"I've never really thought about it."

"Although I guess if you kept it a planet you'd have to make Eris a planet too. Maybe even Haumea and Makemake. I mean, once you start naming planets, where do you make the cutoff point?"

"I really have no idea. I also have no idea why you listen to music about people killing each other in the ghetto."

Martin rolled his eyes. "It's called the hood."

"It's called the place people should try to get out of, not glorify."

Martin struck a pose that was supposed to look gangsta. "It's cool."

I almost said that he wouldn't last two minutes in

one of those neighborhoods, but decided to skip it. He was happy to see me. That was the main thing.

He rummaged through the heaps of stuff on his floor as the carnage in the bad side of town continued on the airwaves. From beneath a cairn of old socks, discarded athletic gear, and various unidentifiables, he pulled out *Cargo Blasters #4: Passage to Pluto*. The shiny bright cover showed three teens, two boys and a girl, driving spaceships that looked an awful lot like eighteen-wheelers with rockets attached. Pluto hung in the background, along with several menacing UFOs that I knew from previous install-ments were the ships of the G.R.U.B.S., which stood for Grotesque Repulsive Unsanitary Bug-Eyed Species. The aliens were the main bad guys of the series. The artwork was marred on one corner with a ketchup stain. At least I think it was ketchup.

"Thank you," I said, holding it with two fingers as I gingerly placed it in my purse. "I'll get right on it."

"So, have you bought my birthday present yet?" Martin asked, kicking a pile of Lego pieces.

"You really need to learn the art of subtlety."

"What's that?"

"Never mind."

"So, what did you get me?"

"Something cool and modern."

"Something street?"

"I can't afford an entire street, not on my pension."

That earned me a teenaged eye roll. It was a bad joke, so I suppose I deserved it.

"The birthday party is on Friday at seven."

"I remember your birthday, Martin."

"That's the day after tomorrow."

"I know."

"We're having it at the indoor skate park."

"I know, I know."

"We'll be skating before then, but you don't have to come for that."

"Why not? They have beginner's classes. Maybe I should try."

That earned me another eye roll.

"Let's go get some ice cream," he said, clambering over the wreckage that was his living space. "I think Mom and Dad left some in the freezer."

I smiled and followed him. Hopefully I'd have this mystery solved in the next couple of days so I could enjoy celebrating Martin turning fourteen with a clear mind and a sense of accomplishment.

That night, with a cup of tea by my side and my tortoiseshell kitten, Dandelion, curled up on my feet,

I checked the Internet for everything I could find on the late, great Sir Edmund Montalbion.

I found quite a lot.

First off, I discovered that the "sir" was an actual title from England. He was English, although he had lived much of his life in the United States, and he had earned his knighthood for "services to the realm." The services turned out to be acting as a go-between to land several lucrative mining deals for British businesses in Africa and Asia. These were all gemstone mines, diamonds mostly. Thanks to him, the English had taken a bite of the diamond industry, something that had been dominated by the Belgians for many decades.

I thought they only gave out knighthoods for slaying dragons or saving damsels in distress. I didn't know you could get knighted for making private corporations oodles of cash, but what did I know about knights?

These deals had no doubt made him oodles of cash, too, although reading between the lines of his life story, that never seemed to be his primary motivation. He never created his own business, although he certainly had the capital and knowledge to do so, and he never stayed as a consultant with any one company for long. Much of his time was spent at gem shows and auctions in every important capital in the world. He was renowned for his personal collection of rare gems, many of which had stories attached to them.

For example, a couple of years ago he had spent $3.2 million at an auction at Christie's to buy an emerald-and-ruby diadem that had been owned by the wife of one of India's richest maharajas in the nineteenth century. This diadem had been the target of an ingenious plan by some of the maharaja's servants, who had decided to steal it. Knowing that they would be suspected if it went missing, and not wanting to live their lives on the run, they hired a master jeweler to make an exact replica with crystal stones instead of real ones.

The plan would have worked, too, except the jeweler did his job too well. What he didn't know was that the maharani (that's a female maharaja, something I didn't know until I read this story) had dropped the diadem and snapped one of the delicate gold threads. Because of this, the frayed end always jabbed her in the scalp when she put it on. But as the old saying goes, it is better to look good than to feel good, and she would wear the prickly diadem on all state occasions. She was too afraid of her husband,

GRANNY GOES ROGUE    55

who had quite a temper, to tell him that she had dropped it.

The next time she put it on, however, she noticed there was no snapped gold thread. She immediately guessed the truth and told her husband, who proceeded to show his renowned temper to the servants in quite a bloody manner. Several hot irons and a bath of boiling water later, he wrung a confession from the few servants still remaining alive and learned where the real diadem was hidden.

Quite the history, and our murder victim lapped it up, so much so that he even bought the fake diadem for $500,000, even though the value of its materials was barely worth a tenth of that.

Sir Edmund Montalbion was a collector through and through. He was reputed to have a sample of every gemstone known to man, and even every gemstone known to woman, which is a considerably greater number.

His most recent acquisition was one of his rarest, and most expensive. It was the Volcano Stone of Panama, an immense fire opal. While fire opals are beautiful red gemstones, they tend not to be as expensive as, say, diamonds, but this one was incredibly pure and was the largest cut fire opal in the world, weighing in at twelve thousand carats. It was also unusual in that it was the only fire opal ever to be found in Panama. Fire opals are rare in Guatemala and Honduras, and not found any further south until you get to Brazil. This unusual feature added to its value. He bought it on a private purchase so the details were sketchy, but the estimated market value was well over $1 million.

So the obvious motive for murdering Sir Edmund Montalbion was to rob him, but what was the motive for dumping him in the highly secure building of a big-box store?

So far, I couldn't find one. I did find several specialist Internet forums and collectors' newsletters where he spoke out against SerMart, saying they were a "travesty on the gemstone trade" and "the jewelry equivalent to a fast-food hamburger."

Perhaps putting his body in SerMart was some sort of act of humiliation? Seemed a bit of a stretch, considering the danger involved. And it wasn't like he was the only person complaining about Serengeti.com. Lots of people hated them for edging out small retailers and even midsized chains. There had even been antitrust lawsuits, complaining that the corporate giant was acting as a monopoly. Those had all been ruled in Serengeti.com's favor, however.

It wasn't a monopoly; it was just huge and getting huger.

I finished my tea and put my computer to sleep. I had gotten as far as I could with online research. The next step was to start making inquiries on the ground, especially within the business community.

Luckily, I had a date with a member of the business community the very next morning.

# SIX

Octavian was well-dressed as usual. He had changed from his bright summer suits to a dark blue for the autumn season, his tie on just right and his shirt freshly pressed. An important businessman in the city until his retirement, he had not let his wardrobe get any more casual.

The formality of his dress was at odds with his character, which was warm and open. He never had a cross word for anybody unless they deserved it, like if they were trying to kill the both of us. He was one of the few civilians who knew I had worked for the CIA. I hadn't intended on telling him, but it sort of came up during the whole "the Mob is trying to kill us" phase of our relationship. He got lots of brownie points for sticking around after that.

We sat at the Tic Toc Café, one of Cheerville's more popular, and noisy, eateries. We came for the crepes, which were the best I've ever tasted. They were so good, in fact, that we were willing to endure the café's vast collection of clocks. Every wall was covered in them, and every corner had a grandfather clock standing in it. Even our table was a big, round clock on its back, the hands ticking away time half obscured beneath our plates and coffee cups. I took it all as symbolic. Two lovebirds on the wrong side of seventy enjoying each other's company while the cold hand of time ticked relentlessly toward the moment of their mutual doom.

Sorry, that was a bit glum. Murders in retail outlets tend to affect my emotions in adverse ways.

So, we sat and talked amid the ticking and the tocking, trying to ignore the passage of time. Ignoring the passage of time had become much easier since Octavian had come into my life.

And yet despite the wonderful company, my mind kept drifting to the sight of that poor man lying in my shopping cart with a knife through his head.

Octavian put down his fork. "You seem distracted."

I blinked and looked at him. I had the vague

sense that he had said something before this, but for the life of me I couldn't remember what.

"Oh, it's just getting everything organized for Martin's birthday. I got him a gift, but you know how kids are. So picky..."

My boyfriend cocked his head and studied me for a moment. "No, it's more than that."

"Really, it's nothing you need to worry about."

He picked up his fork and began to eat again, lost in thought. There was a silence at the table that I couldn't quite break. Suddenly, Octavian sat bolt upright.

"Aha!" he shouted, pointing his fork at me with such force that a portion of crepe flew off the end of it and landed on my plate.

"Yes, I'd love some crepe. Thank you."

Octavian blushed. "Oh, sorry. But I've figured out what it is." He looked around at the other tables then leaned forward and in a conspiratorial whisper said, "It's another case, isn't it?"

"Really, Octavian, I—"

He waggled his fork at me. "Come on, now. You can't hide this from me. I've seen you on three cases before this one, and I can tell when you're on the hunt."

Yes, he actually used the term "on the hunt," as if

I was some sort of bounty hunter. I got offered that job once, and while the pay was tempting, I preferred the travel that the CIA offered me. I mean, who doesn't want to do forced marches through the Salvadoran jungle?

I sighed and then told him the whole story. He would have wheedled it out of me eventually.

"SerMart," he said once I finished. "There's a coincidence. Albert just got a job there."

"Who?"

"You know, Albert. The stoner waiter who caught you with a dead body in the Cheerville Country Club men's room."

"Do keep your voice down. I like this café and want to be able to come back to it. Why would Albert be working at SerMart? He seemed to like his job at the country club."

Mostly because it gave him plenty of opportunity to smoke pot and race golf carts around the grounds with his fellow underachievers.

"Oh, he got fired. Drugs."

"Well, I can't say I'm surprised."

"No, he wasn't taking drugs. He's stopped now. He caught a businessman snorting cocaine in the men's room, and the guy reported on him."

"Why would the businessman report him? Shouldn't it be the other way around?"

"Well, Albert's not the reporting kind. This businessman, though, has a lot of influence. He was worried that Albert would try to blackmail him and so made up a story about Albert sneezing into his gin and tonic."

I shook my head. "The more I learn about this town, the more I want my old job back."

At least drug kingpins and terrorists were honest about who they were.

"It's almost as ugly as the city at times," Octavian said, nodding sadly. "So after Albert lost his job, I helped him get one at SerMart."

"That doesn't seem like his sort of place."

"Why not? He's a modern kid, and they're so innovative and cutting-edge."

"Ugh." I put my head in my hands.

"What's the matter?"

"Nothing. Do go on."

"So he's been there for a week now. He replaced someone who got fired. Imagine that? The store has only been open a couple of weeks, and they have already let somebody go."

"You can't get good help these days. I'm still surprised Albert took that job. They're pretty heavy on the rules, and I'm sure they do drug tests."

"Oh, he's a changed kid. Our little adventure with the murder in the country club really woke him up. He doesn't smoke dope anymore, and he's taking business classes part-time at Cheerville Community College."

"How do you know so much about what he's doing?"

"I've been helping him get on his feet. He's still a bit disorganized," Octavian said with a chuckle.

"Well, that's nice of you, but why take such an interest in some millennial who can't string together a coherent sentence half the time?"

Octavian grew serious. "Because I hate to see wasted potential. Remember how he helped us in that case? I saw a bright mind under all that marijuana-induced fog, and a sense of honor too. All he needed was a good kick in the pants. He obviously wasn't getting it from his own parents."

I reached over and put my hand on his.

"You're a good man, Octavian."

My words got drowned out as all the clocks in the café suddenly rang eleven. The café reverberated with a cacophony of bonging, clonging, ringing, buzzing, chiming, and trumpeting. Yes, trumpeting.

A clock in the shape of a castle rang out the hours by having the drawbridge pop open to reveal three little trumpeters in medieval livery, who proceeded to trumpet eleven times with their tiny, tinny instruments.

We didn't even try to talk. We had learned our lesson from previous visits. Only a megaphone could cut through this din, and I didn't have a megaphone in my purse. A set of lockpicks, yes. Pepper spray, of course. Pistol, on special occasions. But no megaphone.

The bonging, clonging, ringing, buzzing, chiming, and trumpeting finally died down. The drawbridge snapped shut, hopefully sending those annoying little trumpeters straight to the dungeon.

We waited. After about twenty seconds, Octavian pointed across the room at a cuckoo clock.

He was right on the money. The moment he pointed at it, a little yellow bird popped out of the clock and cuckooed the time.

"They still haven't fixed that thing," he grumbled.

"Can you give me Albert's number?" I asked. "I'd like to speak with him."

Octavian checked his watch, a refined antique Rolex from 1936, and said, "We're in luck. We have just enough time to finished these wonderful crepes and drive over to the community college. He'll be getting out of his Economics 101 class pretty soon."

We took Octavian's car, which is much classier than mine, and enjoyed a pleasant drive through town—past the spot where I saw someone get run over by "accident," past the village green where someone tried to kill a movie star with a barrage of fireworks, past a strip mall at the edge of town where gangsters had set up an illegal casino and tried to kill me when I exposed it. Oh yes, a very pleasant drive through a tranquil, prosperous community. The kind of place where successful people move to raise their families in peace and security.

I had never been on the campus of Cheerville Community College. It looked like a pretty typical small-town college with several low brick buildings, a leafy quad where students sat on the grass studying or flirting, and young people strolling along paths or whizzing by on their bicycles.

Albert was waiting for us in front of one of the buildings, Octavian having called with the promise of a free lunch. No college student will pass up a free lunch. When Albert spotted us, he gave a friendly wave.

"Dude! How's it hanging?"

Octavian checked his tie. "Fine, I think."

Albert chuckled, shaking his head and turning to me. "He's hopeless. So, how's life with you? Finding any more dead bodies in the men's room?"

"No, just one in my shopping cart."

He laughed then looked at me, and the laughter slowly died away. "Oh. You mean it."

I sighed. "It would be nice if you thought I was joking."

"No way, grandma. Not with you. Octavian told me how you two almost got beaten to death by bowling balls on your cruise."

"You shouldn't tell him things like that," I said to my boyfriend.

He shrugged. "I don't want him to think I have a boring life."

"Just a mostly boring one," Albert said.

"Watch it, or you'll talk your way out of a free lunch."

"I got a study group coming up in 45 minutes, so let's eat on campus. There's a good pizza place in the student union."

As we walked there, I studied Octavian and Albert chattering away. My boyfriend had obviously taken on the role of the caring grandfather figure.

And this underachieving druggie was lapping it

GRANNY GOES ROGUE    67

up and turning his life around. It was remarkable how just a little bit of attention and guidance could make such a difference in a young person's life.

It made me wonder about all those people I've killed over the years, all those so-called "bad guys." They weren't the faceless aliens of Martin's young adult science fiction novels. They had been children once, and at some point, they had gone wrong. The drug dealers, the henchmen for brutal dictators, even that assassin who had come after me, they had all had the chance to be someone better.

If only there were more Octavians in the world...

We ended up at the student union in a loud, echoing cafeteria filled with college kids. Octavian and I were the oldest people in sight by several decades. Since we had just eaten, we only got coffees (bad ones) while Albert got a large Hawaiian pizza.

"Mixing pepperoni with pineapple is a sin against nature," Octavian said with a frown.

"No way, dude. It's, like, diversity."

"Segregation was wrong, but I might make an exception for such a travesty of the taste buds."

Albert plopped down a class schedule.

"After we eat, I need to ask you what I should take next term."

I picked up the list of classes and leafed through

it. Besides the typical ones I was familiar with like economics and biology, there were strange ones I had never heard of, like Exobiology and Intersectional Justice Studies. I had no idea what exobiology was. Justice Studies was probably something to do with law enforcement, but what did "intersectional" mean? Maybe bringing all the forces together to cooperate? That would be good. The FBI, CIA, DoD, ATF, and all the other acronyms were too territorial, not wanting to share intelligence with each other in case another bureau nabbed the bad guys and got all the credit.

I put the class catalog down and decided to get down to business.

"I heard you work at SerMart."

Albert rolled his eyes in a good imitation of my grandson, who was ten years younger.

"Way boring place. Totally corporate. Except yesterday! Some dead dude fell off the shelves and straight into some little old lady's shopping cart. She screamed so loud everyone thought she was getting murdered. She even peed herself." Albert looked at me. "Oh wait... didn't you say you had a body in your shopping cart? Wait. That was you?"

Albert may have been off pot, but he was still a bit slow on the uptake.

"Young man, I did not pee myself."

"Glad to hear it," Octavian said.

Albert looked from me to Octavian and back again.

"So... um, this pizza isn't free, is it?"

"Not exactly, no." I admitted. "Can you tell me if you've seen anything unusual going on at SerMart?"

"Besides the flying drones that never shut up and all the weird rules?"

"Yes, besides those."

Albert shrugged. "Nothing that I've seen. I mean, everyone hates it there, but why kill a dude? I heard he was up on the shelves and came falling down. I sure didn't see any dead bodies when I was up there, and I had the late shift, midnight to six a.m."

I put down my coffee. "Wait, you were there the night of the murder?"

"Totally."

"I reviewed the camera footage for that shift and looked closely at every face. I didn't see you there."

"Really? Maybe you need to get your prescription checked."

"My prescription is just fine. Did you go up to the catwalk from the door in the back room?"

"Yeah. That's the only way to get up there,

except for the freight elevator, but mostly the loading dock crew just fills the elevator with stuff and we take it out up top."

Octavian scratched his head, which was still attractively covered with a full mop of hair. Gray, of course, but at least not bald.

"And you're not on the video? That doesn't make any sense."

"It does if someone altered the video," I said.

"It looks like we have a very clever murderer to find," Octavian said.

"What do you mean 'we'?"

Octavian grinned, showing a set of well-preserved teeth. "Well, I can't let my life get boring, can I?"

## SEVEN

Police Chief Arnold Grimal did not look happy to see me. That was normal. If he ever looked happy to see me, I knew to be on my guard because he was cooking something up in that little pea brain of his.

His desk was strewn with paperwork and Chinese takeaway boxes. As I came in, he was just finishing off some lemon chicken, wielding his chopsticks with the dexterity of a Shaolin monk.

At least he was good at something.

"Crack the case yet?" I asked. That was me cracking a joke.

His eyes hooded, and he looked into the depths of his takeaway box.

"We're following several leads," he mumbled.

"Such as?" I asked, sitting down. He hadn't

invited me to sit, which is why I sat. It was good to remind him who was boss.

"The servants. He had several, and two of them, the cook and the butler, slept at his house in the servants' quarters. They had opportunity and motive. We had his accountant come in and go through his collection. One of his prize gemstones is missing."

"Which one?"

"Something called the Volcano Stone of Panama. Apparently it's worth a cool million bucks. I knew robbery was the motive."

"No, it wasn't."

Grimal tossed his chopsticks into the takeaway box with an angry gesture, making some lemon sauce fly out and hit his lapel. It blended with the yellow suit and was barely noticeable. Maybe that's why he wore yellow suits.

"Oh, come on! Someone takes a million-dollar opal, and you say robbery wasn't the motive?"

"A fire opal," I corrected, "and robbery obviously wasn't the motive, or at least not the primary motive. You didn't mention anything else missing."

Pause. "No. That was the only thing that was stolen."

"Where was the fire opal kept?"

"In a display case. Bulletproof glass, security alarm. Someone obviously had the key."

Or knew how to hack a security system, like I did.

"Anything else in the display case?"

"A bunch of other gemstones."

"Bingo. And they were all still there, weren't they?"

"Well, yes, but they were less valuable. Maybe someone was commissioned to steal only that stone. It happens with art thieves."

"Art is easier to trace. Unscrupulous collectors who want a particular work of art will commission thieves to steal it and then keep it hidden in their private residence. You can always cut gemstones to make them impossible to recognize. I doubt a thief would pass by some valuable stones when they would only take a few seconds to grab. Even if they were commissioned to take the fire opal, why not steal some more stones to add to their profits and make it less obvious that the Volcano Stone was the target? Any signs of violence in the house?"

"Yes, we found traces of blood in his bathroom. It's a private bathroom off the master bedroom. The killers tried to clean up but left a few traces of blood on the wall and in the bathtub. Forensics thinks he was killed there, because the traces on the wall look like spray from the exit wound. They think his body was then drained of blood and washed and dressed in the tub, which was then rinsed clean, or almost clean. The linen closet was missing almost all the towels. I suppose the murderer used them to clean up and then disposed of them."

"Were his wallet and keys on his bedside table?"

Grimal nodded.

"How much was in the wallet?"

"A couple of hundred. None of the credit cards were missing."

I sat back and thought. So whoever did this got access to a very well-protected mansion, got into Sir Edmund's room, and killed him in his bathroom in the wee hours of the morning. Grimal started showing me crime scene photos. The mansion was a big one, elegantly furnished. The walls were of brick with oak flooring. The servants' quarters were on the floor above the master bedroom. With the two servants fast asleep at that hour, it was quite possible that they would not have heard a scuffle or even the victim getting stabbed. There was only one wound, and that would have killed him instantly.

There probably wasn't much of a struggle. Sir Edmund's knuckles were scuffed, perhaps from punching his assailant. Given the strength of the attacker, I doubt that would have slowed him or her down. The fight would have been a quick one.

Did the victim scream? Perhaps he was too surprised or frightened to scream. That often happened when people faced mortal danger. I'd seen that in the field all too many times.

So the servants might have slept through the whole thing. They might have woken to the unusual sound of running water in the early hours of the morning, but there would be no reason why they would investigate that.

But what about the burglary alarm? And the locks? And the dogs?

As if reading my thoughts, Grimal said, "It had to be an inside job. Only the servants could have gotten through the security system. The outside servants, the gardener and the two maids, don't have the security codes for the alarm system. They have to be let in every morning by the butler or the cook, or by Montalbion himself. One or both of them crept downstairs, killed him, washed his body, and disposed of his bloody pajamas. We still haven't found those. Then they went to SerMart, got in somehow, and dumped the body."

"Did either servant have any bruises?"

"You mean from the victim punching someone? No, they didn't, but the guy wasn't exactly Muhammad Ali."

True enough. "What have you learned from the butler and the cook?"

Grimal shrugged. "Not much. They both claim they didn't hear anything that night, and when the butler knocked on Montalbion's bedroom door at eight o'clock in the morning to announce breakfast was served, he didn't get a response. He waited half an hour then knocked again. When he didn't get a response a second time, he opened the door and found Montalbion missing."

"But he didn't report him missing."

"He claimed that he assumed his master went out for a walk, which he did sometimes, although it was odd for him not to say anything to them first. The butler called around to various neighbors, who hadn't seen him. We checked on that with the neighbors and found that was true, but of course that could have been a dodge. I think the butler did it."

Well, that was an original conclusion.

"Did he call the police to report a missing person?"

Grimal sat up, a proud look on his face. "No, he did not."

"He must have noticed the wallet and keys on the nightstand and wondered why his boss would go out without them."

"Yeah, that's even more proof! He slipped up with that one."

The eagerness with which Grimal leapt on this idea showed he hadn't thought of it himself.

"What about the cook?" I asked.

"The knife used in the murder was identical to a set from the kitchen. That one was missing, so it's obviously the same one. I don't think the cook did it, though. Oh, she might be an accomplice, but she's not the murderer. She's a little old lady. No way she... could..."

Grimal's voice trailed off when he saw how I was looking at him.

"How strong is the butler?" I growled.

"He's in his thirties, a healthy thirties. Hardly gargantuan, but he looks strong enough."

"Strong enough to put a knife through a man's skull?"

"Maybe in a fit of rage. Adrenaline can do a lot for a man."

"Like you'd know," I muttered.

"I'll have you know I was quite fit in my earlier

days," he grumbled, fishing around for the last of his lemon chicken.

"Did you know the security video was altered?" I asked.

That got him to look up.

"Really? And how would you know that?"

"I know an employee who was there the night before Sir Edmund made his dramatic appearance. He went through that door in the back room and up to the catwalk. I didn't see him in the tape. They must have replaced the real footage with footage from a previous night."

"Maybe you need a new prescription," Grimal said. "And don't call it tape. It's all computerized now. Nobody uses videotape anymore."

"A figure of speech, like saying you're reading the newspaper when you're reading online."

"Nobody says that either. Just say you're reading the news."

I frowned. "If I wanted a lecture on modern English usage, I'd ask my grandson. In any case, we have to figure out who altered that tape."

"Computer file."

"Stop. The murderer is obviously an employee, or has an accomplice who is an employee. What I don't understand is how they managed to drop the body on me and get away unseen."

"That's a strange one," the police chief admitted. "The butler is the obvious culprit. We're holding both servants for questioning. Maybe we can get them to confess who they were working with at SerMart."

"Let's go question them, then," I said, standing up. My back gave a sharp stab, and I hissed in agony.

"You all right?" Grimal asked.

"It's nothing." What the heck was causing that?

"You can't question the suspects," he said. "It's against procedure."

"Shall I call my former boss?"

I had scared him with the CIA director before. It always worked.

This time, it didn't.

Grimal tapped his chopsticks impatiently on the desk, leaving little lemony dots all over a case file. "Think about it. You were the first person to find the body. You might have even been intended as the second victim. If you question the suspects and they go to trial, their lawyer will make a big deal about it. They'll say the police investigation was biased."

Hmm. He had me there. Grimal was definitely getting better at this whole police-work thing. He was almost at the level of a rookie in his first month of basic training.

I found it irritating.

He found it exhilarating.

Treating me to a smug smile, he said, "Don't worry, they're in good hands. I'm sure I'll wring a confession out of them quickly enough. Why don't you go play shuffleboard or something?"

Oh, those were fighting words.

"I'll drop by if I have any questions," I said. "And I'll inform you when I crack the case."

I turned and left in a huff.

The problem was, I didn't know where to start the investigation.

I did know the first thing I needed to do, though, and that was go home and take an aspirin and a piping hot bath.

Nothing like relaxing the muscles to get the brain working. First off, I called Albert. It took three tries to get him.

"Whaaaah?" he said.

I could hear sitar music playing in the background.

"Albert, this is Barbara Gold. I was wondering if you are working the night shift at SerMart tonight."

My question was answered with loud coughing.

"Are you smoking?" I asked.

"Huh? Uh, no. No! I just, like, got a cold and stuff."

"Are you working the night shift tonight?" I asked the question slowly, enunciating my words to cut through the fog. It looked like poor Octavian put too much faith in the boy.

"Yeah, totally I'm working. The midnight to six shift. I'm about to take a nap. It's hard working nights, you know."

"My heart bleeds for you. I want you to keep your eyes open, you hear? I'll call you while you're on the job and ask you to do some things for me."

"No way, José. We're not allowed to have cell phones at work."

I groaned. "Oh, of course you're not. Bring it anyway."

"The cameras will see."

"Not when you're up on the catwalk. Put it on vibrate so no one hears it, and only answer if you're up there and out of sight."

"Um, okay. Like, what are you going to have me do?"

"I'll tell you when the time comes. Now stop smoking, and take a nap to clear your head."

"Okay, grandma."

He hung up.

The truth was, I didn't know what I was going to have him do, but having a man on the inside (or a brain-addled half boy) could be a great asset. I didn't see how I could get in there myself. While I could bypass the alarm, the cameras would spot me, and so would the employees.

At the moment, Albert was the only person I had to work with. Grimal was quite right in telling me that I couldn't interview the suspects or be seen conducting an investigation considering that I may have been directly involved. Of course, he was only telling me that to get me to go away.

Fat chance.

I needed to figure out a way to get close to the case without seeming to, and using someone a little more useful than a red-eyed twentysomething.

But then I got a surprise break from the person I least expected.

Police Chief Grimal himself.

## EIGHT

"The surveillance video at the house has been altered too," Grimal told me by phone later that day.

"Really?"

"A clip has been taken out of about two hours from one to three in the morning. It was replaced with footage of empty grounds."

"Don't say 'footage.' That's an old term from the days of film. Everything is electronic now."

"Har har. You want to be filled in on this case or not?"

I did. But I wasn't sure why he was telling me anything. I thought he wanted me as far away from the case as possible.

"All right. Fill me in."

"We had a computer expert look at it and at the

surveillance recordings at SerMart. Both were deleted and replaced with earlier footage via an external server. What server we don't know, because they masked that with something called a VPN. That stands for..." I heard a rustle of papers on the other end of the line. "... a virtual proxy network. Apparently, you can run your Internet access through a bunch of servers in various countries, making it almost impossible to trace you. Whoever did this used a secure wiping program that makes it impossible to recover the deleted video."

"Do you have any idea who did it?"

"That's where you come in."

"Well, I didn't do it. I didn't even know what a VPN was until you told me."

I could practically hear the eye roll on the other end of the line. A wet, squishy sound of utter exasperation. I love that sound.

"Of course you didn't. I mean, I want you to use your, um, connections to find out who did. We think it happened via the security company that monitors the video. Both SerMart and Montalbion's mansion were covered by Escudo Security. We can get a warrant, but it will take time, and they might still be trying to cover their tracks. Your... friends... in government can get into their system quicker."

"All right. I'll make a few calls."

"Thanks."

I blinked. That thank-you sounded genuine.

"That will be all I'll need you for at the moment," Grimal said with an officious tone.

Well, he just ruined that, didn't he?

He hung up without saying goodbye.

Humph. Well, at least it was an interesting lead.

Then a little bell went off in my head. "Escudo" means "shield" in Spanish. I checked Escudo Security's website. Besides the usual sales pitches and details of services, there was a page with employee names and photos. All the senior positions, and most of the junior ones, were taken by Hispanics. The bio of the company president, Ricardo Morales, said he was born in Mexico and immigrated to the United States at an early age. Similar statements were made by several other employees.

I wondered about that. They all had a distinctive look to them—broad faces, flat and wide noses, straight black hair cropped close. They looked like they all had a large amount of Native American blood in them. Of course, that's true of many people in Mexico, but it tends to be more common in southern Mexico. That look is much more common in the Central American countries further south.

Like Panama.

And the only gemstone missing from Sir Edmund's vast and priceless collection was the Volcano Stone of Panama.

Well, wasn't that an interesting coincidence?

CIA operatives don't believe in coincidence.

And back in the 1980s, my late husband, James, and I had been assigned to several missions in Panama. Manuel Noriega, once a U.S. ally and one of the only Latin American leaders not to have ties to the Soviet Union, had gotten his hands dirty with drug trafficking and had been making overtures to the Soviets. We had gone on several missions to break up his drug network and recruit military officers to overthrow him. I was probably the only person in Cheerville who had been in Panama during those tense days, and whose shopping cart did Sir Edmund Montalbion fall into?

That made two coincidences I didn't believe in.

I put in a call to the CIA. Yes, I had retired a few years ago, but like the Mafia, no one leaves the Company. I still occasionally got calls asking for advice, and as a professional courtesy, I could do the same.

The person I was looking for was Gary Wycliff. Gary had been a cub agent back in the eighties, all bright-eyed and bushy-tailed. Nearly got killed on his first mission with us, which dulled his eyes and drooped his tail somewhat. He learned, though, and survived a lot of hard assignments until a bit of Taliban shrapnel gave him a permanent limp and a desk job in Langley, Virginia.

He also had undying loyalty to me because James saved his life once. He saved James's life once, too, but that didn't make it even. That's not how it works.

"Barbara Gold! How are you? It's been too long."

"Oh, things are going about the same as usual"—yes, witnessing a murder was the "same as usual" for me—"and how are you, Junior?"

Gary laughed. "I turned fifty-six last month! I guess I'll never get rid of that nickname, will I?"

"When you started with us, you only had to shave once a week."

"Ah, the good old days."

After a bit more chatter, we got down to business. Soon I could hear him tapping away on the CIA's computer database.

"Ah, here we go. Escudo Security. Yep, it's just as you suspected. The company is co-owned by the president, vice president, and accountant. All three of them came in on Mexican passports but are in fact Panamanian. They are now all green-card holders."

"If we know that their passports were fake, why did we let them in?"

"Because we gave them to them."

"Oh. May I ask why?"

"That's classified."

"Come on now, Junior. I explained the situation. I might be a target here."

"I know, and I'm sorry. It's above your level. You know how it works."

I did. A CIA agent didn't have free access to every bit of information the agency had. We operated on a need-to-know basis. I'd been out for a while, and while my service was respected and got me a lot of perks, it did not give me a look at everything they were doing.

Especially if it had to do with an ongoing project or something that occurred after my retirement.

But was it? While the CIA kept agents in every country in the world, Panama wasn't as hot as it used to be. Noriega was in prison, the Soviet threat was long gone, and the Panama Canal was running smoothly. While the country was more or less stable now, and stably in the orbit of the United States, it still needed watching. All of Latin America did.

Now it wasn't Communist insurgents. Instead it was potential coups by generals who would be hostile to the United States and its interests or the rising power of drug barons. The drug barons were the worst. While dictators always created enemies and rivals and were thus fairly straightforward to topple, drug barons were harder targets. They didn't have a presidential palace to storm or a regiment of troops you could turn to your side. They moved in the shadows and had secret and always-changing distribution networks, and even if you nabbed them, there was always someone eager to take their place.

So what was I dealing with here? Not drug kingpins. Despite the rumors, the CIA didn't deal in drugs. We did occasionally get intel from people in the drug trade so we could take out rivals or people higher up the food chain. Could the people of Escudo Security be some mid-level narcos who informed on their boss and got granted a new life in the United States? If so, they were picking an odd way to lay low. Their pictures were right there on their website.

So this must be more of a government thing. What it was, I couldn't say. None of the faces I'd seen on the Escudo Security website looked over fifty, making them teens or kids during the tumultuous years of the eighties. They wouldn't have been important enough to pull out of the country.

Unless they were the sons of important people.

Gary, bless his heart, kept quiet as all this whirred through my mind. I bet he could hear the wheels turning over the line.

"Could you at least tell me how much danger I'm in?" I asked at last.

Pause. "None if you walk away now. A lot if you keep sticking your nose in it, which I know you will. It's best to let some things lie, Barbara."

"Did I mention the dead body of a multimillionaire falling from a tall height and nearly crushing me?"

"You did. I don't know why they did that. I suppose it was to send a message."

"You mean a warning?"

"No, more of a message. They didn't want to kill you. At least I'm pretty sure they didn't. They obviously wanted you to take notice, though."

"I do wish you would stop being so cryptic, Junior."

"I'm a spy. You're a spy. Cryptic is what we do."

I had to laugh at that. He always was fun to be around.

Something occurred to me.

"I didn't tell anyone I was going to SerMart. I was going for a... surprise present."

I had almost slipped and said it was for Martin. Best to keep him out of it.

"You may not have told your friends or family, but I bet you told SerMart," Gary said.

I blinked. "Why yes, yes, I did. I called the evening before to ask their hours."

"At what time?"

"Around five-thirty."

"And when did you say the murder was?"

"Hours later." Long enough to plan. "So Escudo Security has tapped their phones?"

"Not tapped. It's part of their contract to monitor phone calls to head off any threats. Serengeti.com has a lot of enemies. That's why they bought that service."

I leaned back in my chair, my heart racing. You might think that my heart was racing as a nervous reaction to having my phone conversation listened to and traced by some mysterious Panamanians (later Mexicans, now Americans, really who-knows-whats), but that wasn't quite correct. My heart was racing because I was feeling it again—that old thrill of being in the game.

James once compared it to gambling, a vice

neither of us had ever indulged in. Civilians went in for hollow thrills. If you want a real thrill, act undercover in some third world dictatorship that would just love to throw you into some dank dungeon and torture you for a few years before dumping your mangled body into the sea. Why bet on horses when you can bet on your life, with the stakes not only being that you get to see another sunrise but that you can make a real difference in geopolitics? Why get a vicarious thrill off of television when real action is happening all around you?

And this case had all the real action I had loved in my working years—CIA involvement, shadowy figures, a mysterious death, missing loot, and a chance for me to make a difference.

The question was, a difference with what?

"So are you saying the good folks at Escudo Security wouldn't have involved me at all if I hadn't announced that I was coming to SerMart?"

"I'm not saying anything, Barbara."

And that was that. I didn't get another tidbit of information from him.

I did a little online checking on Escudo Security and found little, just a few mentions of contracts with major companies in the state and some photos of the president, Ricardo Morales, at various functions. Some of the other employees were in the background. The photos on their website were genuine. Whatever they had fled from in Central America, they felt safe enough to be out in public these days.

And why not? They'd been let in by the CIA, after all.

My phone rang again. It was Grimal.

"To what rare circumstance do I owe the honor of receiving not one but two phone calls from you today?" I asked.

"Can it. The fingerprints came back," he said.

"And?"

"The bedroom and bathroom had the fingerprints of the butler and maid all over them, but that proves nothing. It's their job to be in there. None from the cook, which lessens the chance of at least her direct involvement although she could have still been an accessory. And no fingerprints on that label Florence Nightingale yanked off the catwalk. Except hers, of course."

"The way she mangled it, I'm not surprised."

"Yeah, that made me cringe. But here's the kicker."

"What?"

"When we took the body out of your shopping cart, we found another bar-code sticker stuck to the bottom of it, the bar code facing up. And get this—it was for the exact same product."

"Another coincidence. This case seems full of them."

"Yeah, but what does it mean?" His voice came out whiny, pleading. He wanted my help but was too proud to ask.

I wish I knew how to help him. I had no idea of the significance of the stickers either.

I had to hope Albert would come up with something on his night shift. I called him just before he went to work to remind him of his duties and fill him in on all the details of the case so he would know what to look for. He had forgotten everything I had told him earlier, of course, but at least he seemed sober now.

"How did you ever pass the drug test?" I asked him. "Surely a company as security conscious and controlling as SerMart would have made you take a drug test."

Albert laughed. "Those are easy to fool! There's a drink you can get at smoke shops that takes it right out of your system. Chug a bottle of that a couple of days before your test and you're home free."

"I see," I said, nettled that he knew something

about the darker side of life that I didn't. "How does it work?"

"Some sort of chemical thing. How should I know? Makes you pee like a Russian racehorse. I was going to the john like three, four times a—"

"That's quite all right. I don't need to know the details. Just remember to keep your eyes open at work, all right?"

"Sure, grandma. I'll call you if I see anything weird."

And he did. He woke me up at one o'clock in the morning, but he was good to his promise.

# NINE

His voice came at such a low whisper I could barely hear what he was saying.

"Hey, grandma. There's, like, something weird going down at SerMart."

I rubbed my eyes and turned on the bedside lamp. My back twinged in protest of being forced to move after a few hours of lying still.

"What's that?" I asked, keeping my voice low so it wouldn't carry too far on his end.

"There's some people who came up from the loading dock I haven't seen before. Usually, nobody comes up on the freight elevator, but these three Mexican dudes came up, and they've been doing stuff around where you said the body fell from."

"What are they doing?" I shifted in bed, propping a pillow under me to try to relieve my back.

"Dunno. They've been moving boxes, but I don't think they're actually working. It's, like, two of them keep moving stuff, but they seem to be doing that to keep anyone from seeing what the third one is doing."

"How long have they been there?"

"Only a couple of minutes. I ducked out and got away to call you. Oh, gotta go. Manager's coming."

The phone cut off.

I was in my car and driving to SerMart in less than five minutes.

It doesn't take long to get ready when you sleep with your clothes on. I didn't sleep with my shoes on, though. I am retired, after all.

I had even left a bottle of painkillers in the glove compartment. I popped one. It reminded me of the time when I had typhoid in the Western Sahara and I had to march twenty miles through the desert. I just dealt with the pain and soldiered on.

Cheerville is a sleepy town, and it's even sleepier at night. The empty streets gave me a chance to calm my quick breathing and take stock of the situation.

We had three "Mexicans" coming into the building and doing something right where the body had been lying. Obviously, these were my Panamanian friends. They probably got access to the loading dock by showing their Escudo Security badges. No one would have questioned that. But what were they doing? Cleaning up the scene? Shouldn't they have done that already?

They must have left something there. Something they didn't want us to find.

The question was, had we already found it or not?

I felt that prickly little thrill I always got when I was hot on the trail of a case. This time, though, it was ten times as strong. This time, it wasn't some local mafia or jealous rival crossing the line into violence. This time, it was international. This time, the CIA was involved somehow.

Which brought back something that had nagged me ever since I had spoken with Gary Wycliff. He hadn't warned me off the case. Well, he had said I'd be in danger if I pursued it and safe if I didn't, but he knew me well enough to know that was like waving a red flag at a bull. He was assistant head of the Latin American desk now. He ranked me. He could have ordered me to steer clear, and I would have had no choice but to grumble and salute. He hadn't ordered me.

So in effect, he asked me to pursue the case.

But he hadn't told me what it was all about.

There's government work for you.

Parking at SerMart proved to be a problem, not because there weren't enough spots but because there were too many. SerMart was a huge building with an equally huge parking lot. The twenty or so vehicles of the night-shift workers looked forlorn sitting under the harsh lamps in that vast space. If I drove in there, I would stick out like a sore thumb, and the people watching the surveillance cameras were the very people I was trying to spy on.

So I drove past. I had remembered from my one and only visit to the store that another street passed behind it. That street was also a commercial district but was much less built up and had only a few stand-alone shops. If I drove along there, I'd get a glimpse between the buildings of my target.

Yes, I notice these things when I'm out shopping for my grandson. It's called situational awareness, and it's saved my life on a number of occasions.

So I drove around the block and took the street behind SerMart at a much slower speed. Here, the stores were much smaller and stood alone. Some looked like they were old converted homes. All were shut, and I ignored their signs as I peeked through the space between the buildings, past a chain-link fence topped with razor wire, and into the back lot of SerMart.

I only got a few quick glimpses, but they were enough. The gate to the loading dock was open, nearly filled by an eighteen-wheeler that had backed into it, harsh light shining out around it and casting a sinister silhouette.

Parked next to it was a four-by-four with a logo painted on the side. My eyes aren't up to reading at that distance under those light conditions anymore, but I did see a big red shield emblazoned next to the words. That told me all I needed to know.

The Panamanians were still inside.

What to do? I couldn't enter the parking lot, and there was no way to sneak in even for someone of my abilities. I did have one thing working in my favor. I remembered from checking out the security video that the cameras only covered SerMart property. They did not capture the roads around the building. I could circle without being seen and wait for them to come out.

So that's exactly what I did, and I didn't have to wait long.

I only made a couple more slow circles around

the block before I came around back again and my heart did a little flippy-flop.

The Escudo Security four-by-four was no longer parked by the loading dock.

I put the pedal to the metal as much as my practical little suburban two-door would allow me and got back on the main road in front of SerMart. I was rewarded by seeing the Escudo Security truck a block ahead of me.

There was a red light between me and them. I groaned in frustration as I stopped at it and saw them just make the light a block ahead.

My phone rang. It was Albert.

"They, like, left."

"I know that. I've been following them and trailing badly. I might just lose them. Why didn't you call earlier?"

"Like, my manager was around. I don't want to lose Productivity Points!"

"Ugh, this company is driving me bonkers."

"Try working here." Pause. "Sorry I couldn't call earlier. I know I'm a screwup."

Now I felt bad. "You are not a screwup, Albert. But you do undercut yourself. That junk you smoke is keeping you at a dead stop in life."

"I don't smoke junk! I don't touch that stuff."

"Oh, come on, I know you're still smoking marijuana."

"That's not junk."

"What is it? Magical fairy leaves from the gods?" This boy gave me no end of irritation.

He laughed. "You could say that. No, junk is slang for heroin. That's bad stuff, man. I'd never touch that."

"It's all a matter of degree."

"Well, I bet you drink," he said with a whine that would have been more appropriate coming out of my grandson.

"Not to excess, and it never got in the way of my education or career. Now if you'll excuse me, I have some murderers to tail."

I hung up just as the light turned green. The security vehicle was still way ahead.

They continued straight then had to slow as an eighteen-wheeler pulled out of a supermarket and blocked their way. Thank God for late-night delivery trucks.

The four-by-four began to pass. I moved as fast as I dared. I wanted to catch up, but I didn't want to attract attention. I worried that these guys would recognize my vehicle. They had obviously been spying on me. Luckily, the streets of this sleepy town are poorly lit, and trying to identify the make and model of a distant car in poor light in a rearview mirror is not an easy task.

I used the eighteen-wheeler as a shield as I approached, which allowed me to take on greater speed. The next time we got caught by a red light, the security guys were only a block ahead and we had left the supermarket truck behind.

We were on the main business road on the edge of Cheerville, heading out of town. I had already checked the location of their office, and that stood in the opposite direction, so these guys were going somewhere else.

After another couple of blocks, it turned out they were going to a motel.

And not just any motel, but the Show 'n' Tell Motel.

The Show 'n' Tell Motel is infamous among the conservative and staid residents of Cheerville. It has a reputation of being a place for assignations of the paid variety. The evidence for this was the garish neon lighting showing an eye opening and closing, the swimming pool that hadn't been filled since 1967, the general squalor of the building and grounds, and the fact that it stood right next to the On-Ramp Burlesque ("Truckers welcome!").

The On-Ramp Burlesque was so named, I dearly hope, because it stood next to the on-ramp to the Interstate. I did not want to ponder other possibilities. It was understated, a blank concrete facade with no windows and a large sign within view of the highway that carried no suggestive pictures. True to its name, it had parking both for cars and trucks, and several eighteen-wheelers were parked there, their exhausted drivers getting a little diversion from their all-night marathon drives across the country.

You would think that the good citizens of Cheerville would kick up a fuss about these two establishments, and you'd be right. But there was nothing they could do about it because both businesses stood just outside city limits, on state land. Cheerville had tried buying the land specifically so they could zone these two places out of existence, but the state wasn't selling. I suspected bribery at the state level.

As the Escudo Security vehicle pulled into the motel and parked out of sight around one side, I was faced with a similar problem to the one I had back at SerMart. If I parked there I would stick out like a sore thumb—not my vehicle, but me. No one would think anything of a seventy-one-year-old man going to such a dive. People would only wink and nod. But a seventy-one-year-old woman? Not on your life. People would think I was a vengeful wife or an angry Bible-thumper. No one would think I was actually a customer. I couldn't blend in. I would only attract suspicion.

I had never been faced with this particular brand of sexism before, and I couldn't figure out how I felt about it. Somewhere between annoyed and flattered.

The safer option was to park in front of the On-Ramp Burlesque. The Panamanians or whoever they were wouldn't be able to see me. They had gone to the far side of the motel.

I pulled in, parked by a larger vehicle that would partially shield me from view if my targets came around to the front of the motel, and got out.

Just as I did, another car pulled up not too far off, and three young men got out, drunk and laughing. They looked like college kids. They spotted me and stopped, jaws hanging open. One giggled. I frowned.

"What are you doing here?" one of them asked.

I put a hand on my hip and gave them a come-hither look.

"Hey boys, I'm the next act. The Gyrating Granny. Wait till you see my—"

They leapt in the car and peeled out of the parking lot so fast they left a trail of burnt rubber.

I hurried over to the Show 'n' Tell Motel before someone from the strip club kicked me off the premises for hurting their business.

The motel was one of those old places that has a single story with rooms all in a row, each with an identical door and battered old air-conditioning unit that probably doesn't work. The building was built like a giant C, with one wing facing the street and the others running back from it on either side. The security folks were on the opposite side somewhere, out of sight.

I unzipped my purse so I could grab the 9mm pistol inside. I also made sure my reading glasses still hung from my neck. Sad to say, I needed them to see the sights on my pistol. Humiliating, I know, but I was still a crack shot as long as I remembered to wear them.

I also carried my pepper spray in the breast pocket of my sweater just in case I needed to get my point across with a little less assertiveness.

The first problem was the manager's office, a glass-fronted room on the corner closest to me. Sitting inside reading a thick book was a haggard man in a grubby tracksuit with thinning salt-and-pepper hair that desperately needed to be cut. He looked up from over the top of his book and spotted me before I even got onto the property. By the time I had made it from one parking lot to the other, he was out of the office and coming for me.

I put my hand in my purse and opened my mouth to speak, but he spoke first.

"If you find him, get him out of here quietly. I don't want any trouble, and the state troopers are personal friends of mine."

He said this not in a hostile manner but matter-of-factly, like he was telling me the room rates or checkout time. I suspected he had to say this a lot.

I put on my best scandalized-long-suffering-wife frown. "I'll have him out of here before you can say 'excessive alimony!'"

He snickered at that.

"Happy hunting," he said, and turned to go.

Then I noticed what book he was reading. It was *War and Peace*, with a bar code from the Cheerville Public Library.

"You're reading Tolstoy?" I said, surprised.

He turned back, his eyes lighting up.

"I love the Russians. Tolstoy, Turgenev, Lermentov, Solzhenitsyn... theirs are the greatest literary treasures of the world."

"They are nice, especially on cold winter nights. I suppose they were written on cold winter nights, or cold summer nights. But I've always preferred the French."

He took in a breath of air and put his hand on his chest. "Ah yes, Gide, Baudelaire, Anatole France... such prose! Such poetry! Have you read *The Gods are Athirst*?"

I smiled. "I really must be going."

He glanced at the hotel and then back at me. "Oh, right. The cheating husband. Go get him! He had to pay for the room in advance anyway. No refunds. No refunds on the Viagra vending machine either. I'm going to get back to my reading. Books are much more reliable than men."

He headed back to his office. I chuckled and shook my head.

Well, at least that was one less problem tonight.

I walked along the front of the hotel, noticing there were no security cameras. Even if there were, my friend already had his nose firmly buried in a classic of Russian literature. The lights were out on all the rooms I passed, but judging from the noises coming from within, the residents were not asleep.

Once I got to the corner, I paused. Glancing over my shoulder to make sure my friend was still reading, I found that he was actually out of sight, sitting as he was, a bit back from the window. Good.

I peeked around the corner. There were about ten motel rooms along this row. Only one had its light on. The four-by-four from Escudo Security was parked in front. From the dim light of the flickering streetlamp that feebly tried to illuminate this part of the parking lot, I could see there was fresh mud on the side of the vehicle.

Only two other cars were parked on this side. I heard no noise coming from those rooms.

I crept up to the motel room door. The view through the window was completely blocked by a heavy curtain. The sound of low voices came from within.

I reached into my purse and pulled out a stethoscope. Yes, a stethoscope. Very good for listening through walls. Even better for listening through windows, the glass conducting sound waves much better than concrete.

I cupped my fingers around the cold end of the stethoscope and placed them gently on the window before easing the stethoscope into position. Just putting it up to the glass would make a telltale click, and I had a feeling these guys had pretty good situational awareness. It might seem like a small precaution, but small precautions had saved my life, and my mission, on countless occasions.

The sounds from inside the motel room came loud and clear now. I heard several male voices speaking in Spanish. I'm fluent in Spanish, fluent enough to recognize a Panamanian accent when I hear it.

"You marked the spot, right?" someone asked. He sounded older, his voice gravelly from many years of smoking.

"Of course. Just like you asked us to. I even put it in a metal box so the animals wouldn't get it."

"Oh, that was a good idea. Should have thought of that myself. We'll move it to a better location in a couple of days. Want a beer?" Gravelly Voice asked.

"Sure."

I heard the sounds of several aluminum cans being opened.

"To Panama for the Panamanians!" Gravelly Voice said.

"To Panama for the Panamanians!" the others replied. Since they all said it together, it was hard to tell their numbers. At least the three I had followed here. Maybe a couple more.

I cursed myself. I should have counted the number of beers being opened. On second thought, there might be a teetotaler in the crowd.

"I think this all went well," one of the voices said. He sounded young, eager for assurance.

"It did," Gravelly Voice said. "No innocent people hurt."

"If only the Americans were so careful," Young Guy replied.

"You're too young to remember," Gravelly Voice said, sounding irritated. "But I do. The Americans were sloppy. They're always sloppy."

"And we get left cleaning up their mess," another voice grumbled.

"It's always the way," Gravelly Voice said. "At least it's all done now. And in a year, we'll be sitting pretty, counting cash for a good deed."

"Sounds good to me," Young Guy said and laughed.

They then started talking about baseball. Panamanian baseball. I listened in for a while about teams and players I'd never heard of as the conversation became increasingly animated. After a few minutes of this, I realized I wasn't going to get any more information this way. They had buried something (the Volcano Stone of Panama?), marked the spot, and were now celebrating. Why were they going to get money in a year? For selling it? If so, they were smart to wait a year for the investigation into its theft to go cold.

And what was that about doing a good deed and cleaning up America's mess? I hardly saw murdering an English multimillionaire as a good deed, and from my investigations into him, he had never had any formal ties to the U.S. besides residency. He hadn't worked for the government, and none of his business deals had ever been in Panama.

I crept away before anyone saw me. While I was tempted to wait until the door opened so I could stick a gun under the nose of the first man to come out, I didn't trust my reflexes enough to keep control of that situation. I had distinguished at least four voices during the conversation about baseball, and if they decided to resist, things could go sour very quickly.

Besides, I wasn't sure just what was going on yet. It didn't appear that they were planning any more murders or planning to get rid of the stone, so I had a bit of time. If I stuck them up now, they would probably shut their mouths and wait for their lawyers. And with their CIA-approved visas, I might never get to the bottom of this. No, it was better to keep on investigating and see what I could find.

I tried to hurry past the office and avoid conversation with the resident literary scholar, but my back twinged and I had to slow down.

"Where is he?" the night manager called out over his book.

"Having a nervous breakdown in the room," I said, pulling out my phone and waving it over my head. "I snapped some photos of him. Smart phones are a wonder, aren't they? He'll be hearing from my lawyer."

He gave me a thumbs-up. "You go, girl!"

"Oh, and don't mention to him that you saw me. He might try and prove entrapment if he thinks you were in on it."

"Mum's the word, grandmum."

"Sorry for taking away one of your customers."

"Nonsense! Once you divorce him, he'll be here more regularly, although I guess he won't be able to afford the deluxe suite anymore. Divorce is good for business."

I walked away, rubbing my back and shaking my head. What an odd business this man had.

What was odder was the business the Panamanians were getting up to. It wasn't simple robbery, and it didn't seem like simple revenge. This case was getting stranger and stranger.

# TEN

"So, what can I do to help?" my boyfriend asked.

Octavian had called bright and early the next morning, early enough that he woke me up. He knows I generally rise at six, but I tend to sleep in after being out late sneaking around cheap motels next to strip clubs. I decided not to talk about this over the phone and had him come over. I filled him in on the latest events while we sat in my living room, having some English Breakfast tea while Dandelion batted around Octavian's shoelaces like they were especially skinny and resilient mice.

"I don't really see what you can do at this stage," I said. Truth be told, I didn't want him on this case. I didn't want him on any of them. While he had been a great help, all through my career I had tried to keep my professional and private lives separate.

He was having none of it.

"How about I go on over to Escudo Security and pretend to be a customer? I could have them come over to my house, and you could pop out of a closet and stick 'em up."

He actually made his hands into the shape of guns like some little boy playing cowboys and Indians.

I chuckled. "I had the chance to do that last night. I don't think we're at that stage of the investigation."

"Oh yes," he said, shaking a finger at me. "The Show 'n' Tell Motel. I hope no one we know saw you there. It would hurt our reputation."

"We have a reputation?"

"This is a small town. People talk. Everyone has a reputation."

"Oh dear."

Grimal had said something similar. About me being known as the nosy new lady who was always being seen in odd places and with odd people. That could be a problem. I used to be good at keeping a low profile.

"Just let me go over there," Octavian said. "I can

get a good look at the place. Maybe I'll get an idea of what they're up to. I'll wear my best watch and cuff links."

"Why?"

"So I look wealthy. These people are obviously attracted to wealth. I only wish I had some gaudy gemstones to flash."

"That's not your style."

"No, it is not, but business is, and I know my kind. While these folks might be murderers and thieves, they're also businessmen. They'll see a wealthy client well connected to the Cheerville community who wants a security system and will see a good opportunity to make some money."

"They just stole a fire opal worth more than $1 million. Why should they care?"

"I did a bit of research on the prices of security systems. The system they sold to SerMart was worth just as much as that, or more. They didn't steal the gem for the money, or at least that wasn't their primary motivation."

I blinked. "Oh. Now that you say that it makes sense. They didn't steal any other gemstones, after all. But in the motel room they were bragging about how they were going to strike it rich."

"Selling that stone will be a nice bonus, and tax-free, too, I suppose. Panama is a good place to launder money. But they have a midsized, growing business. They won't pass up an opportunity to expand like I'm going to offer them. In the meantime, maybe we can get close enough to them to figure out why they only stole one gem when they could have stolen a king's ransom. Money was obviously not their motive."

I gave him a kiss. "I knew I kept you around for something."

He smiled and straightened his tie. "I thought it was for my dashing good looks."

"That too."

Then I had an idea. "All right, here's what we're going to do. I'll go over to your house—"

"Oh, I like this idea already!"

"Behave. Now let me tell you how this is going to work..."

Later that day, I hid in the front hall closet of Octavian's house, snuggled among his overcoats as I heard the doorbell ring.

Octavian, the clever dear, had left the closet door ever so slightly ajar so that I could hear better.

"Hello, sir. I'm Juan Pablo Endara. I'm here to look over your house and give you a security assessment."

"Nice to meet you, young man. As I told your boss on the phone, I'm worried about burglars. I noticed someone had fiddled with the back door the other night. That's why I called."

I heard footsteps head to the back of the house. That was my cue to sneak out the front.

They would be occupied for a few minutes in the back. To make Octavian's story sound plausible, I had tried to pick his back door with a nail file. He had a pretty good lock that couldn't be picked with a nail file, not even by someone of my abilities, but I gave it a good try. That had left several convincing scratches around the lock and the latch that would have this security expert rubbing his hands with glee and telling his obviously wealthy potential client that someone had tried to break into his house.

Octavian leading him to the back door was his way of signaling that the security man had come alone and the coast was clear. If there had been two of them, or if someone had stayed in the security vehicle, then Octavian would have directed him to the front of the house, where he himself had left footprints in the flower bed next to one of the windows.

If you're going to lie in a potentially life-threatening situation, it's best to cover all the angles.

I slipped out of the closet and eased the door

closed behind me. Octavian's voice could still be heard from the back of the house, two rooms away. He would keep the man occupied there for several minutes. After peeking through a window to make sure the coast was clear, I opened the front door as quietly as I could.

The vehicle parked in Octavian's driveway was not, as I'd hoped, the four-by-four I had followed to the motel. Instead, this was just an ordinary car with the Escudo Security logo emblazoned on the side.

I pulled out a small magnetic radio transmitter from my pocket. I had used these before, and they came in handy. You stuck it on the bottom of a vehicle, and it would transmit the car's GPS coordinates to a special receiver with a range of ten miles. All I had to do was to fix it to a good spot and sneak away. Easy as pie.

Famous last words.

I went to the back of the car, got on my hands and knees, and reached under to place the GPS locator on the undercarriage just next to the trailer hitch.

And that's when my back went out.

There was a sharp click—an actual, audible click —and a spike of pain.

And I couldn't move. I was locked into position.

It wasn't that the pain kept me from moving, although the pain was considerable, but that I literally could not bend my back to get up.

I gritted my teeth and set the GPS. First priority —finish the mission. That was so ingrained in me I didn't even think about it. Once the little device was safely tucked away out of sight, I gingerly lifted one hand and rubbed my lower back.

Even that light contact made me hiss in pain.

Where had this come from? And why did it have to happen now?

I heard a car approach. I tried to move crabwise out of sight, but the pain stopped me before I got two feet. Heart thudding, I watched as a four-door sedan drove slowly down Octavian's street. Mother and father in front, looking ahead. Little girl in back, staring at me. I could see her mouth forming words, her finger pointing. The man in the passenger's seat glanced my way. I grinned at him. He looked uncertainly at me before looking away.

And then they were gone.

That's the good thing about civilians. Most of the time they don't want to get involved. They'll make up a perfectly valid reason in their heads why a little old lady is on her hands and knees in their neighbor's driveway and then go on with their little lives.

Okay, one problem solved. Now to solve the big problem. I had maybe another minute or two. Again, I rubbed my back, ignoring the pain as I felt the golf ball-sized knot of tension right at the base of the spine.

I crab crawled to the back of the car, trying to get out of sight of the house. I could just barely reach the top of the trunk and tried to lift myself up, only to fall back on my hands and knees as another spike of pain shot through me.

I slowed my breathing. Tried to relax. What had I learned in those three Seniors' Yoga classes I took with Octavian? Something about focusing on the muscles. Letting go of your worries. I don't recall them saying much about focusing on a clenched back while worrying about getting spotted by a Panamanian jewel thief.

Time. Maybe all I needed was time. And a hot bath. And a handful of aspirins.

Except I didn't have any of those things.

*Focus on the muscles.* I could hear that yoga teacher say in that soothing, somewhat superior voice of hers. *Feel the tension slipping away. Imagine a golden ball of warm light passing from the crown of your head to the base of your feet, removing all tensions.*

Hey, this was actually beginning to work. The pain was slowly beginning to subside. My muscles relaxed. A feeling of well-being flowed through my body. Why didn't they tell us about the magic golden ball in basic training?

*As the tension falls away from your body—*

The front door opened. The golden ball disappeared.

"So, we'll start planning a security system to suit your needs, sir, and we'll—"

"Oh! How silly of me! I forgot to show you the back porch. I'm very worried about it."

Octavian had the foresight to come out first. He spotted me, turned around, and hustled the fellow back inside.

All the tension was back, times two. The golden ball of magic light was nowhere to be seen. I needed to get out of there. Now.

Another attempt at standing told me that wasn't an option, so I crawled my painful way to some rose-bushes at the front of his house and inched behind them, getting pricked and scraped as I got out of sight.

I was still there, on my hands and knees, five minutes later when Octavian and Juan Pablo Endara emerged from the house. Peeking through the rose-

GRANNY GOES ROGUE    123

bushes, some of the thorns adorned with drops of my blood and shreds of my clothing, I watched as the two men shook hands and Juan Pablo got in his car and drove off.

Once he had driven around the corner and out of sight, Octavian looked around, confused.

"Barbara?"

"Right here, dear."

"Where?"

"Kneeling behind the rosebush."

"Why are you doing that?" he asked, coming over.

"Because I can't stand."

He eventually got me vertical, brought me inside, and put one of those heat packs the athletes use on my back.

"I need them sometimes after a long walk or when the weather turns," he admitted as he arranged the pillows around me on the sofa.

The heat pack, some aspirin, and a hot tea fixed me up, and in an hour I was mobile again.

Turning on the GPS locator, I found the Escudo Security car was at the same coordinates as the office. Well, that didn't tell me much. Once it got moving again, I'd keep an eye on it. I'd already rented a car so they wouldn't be able to spot me by my vehicle, which they might know by sight. It would be nice to know why they were spying on me, but just knowing they were was enough to put me on guard. I felt bad bringing Octavian into this. I didn't want him in danger, but he had volunteered knowing the risks, and he had proven to be a big help already.

I decided not to put him at any more risk and to go back home until the security car made a move.

When I got there, I got the surprise of my life.

## ELEVEN

It took a minute to recognize the balding middle-aged man standing on my front porch. But then I mentally put back the hair, took away the wrinkles, and exchanged the sweater and slacks for camo.

"Junior! What are you doing here?"

Gary Wycliff limped off my porch with a big grin on his face and gave me a hug.

"Ow! Careful. I threw my back out."

"Oh, sorry. Let's go inside and talk."

We both hobbled into the house.

"Well, don't we make a pair," Gary said.

"That we do. Time is not kind. When was the last time we saw each other?"

"At James's funeral."

"Oh, yes," I said quietly. "Yes, that was it."

I brewed him a tea, lost in thought. I tried to focus on the case and the reason why a fellow agent was sitting in my living room getting mauled by my kitten, but my mind kept casting back to earlier times.

Gary hadn't been the only agent we had worked with, but he had been one of the best and certainly the best who was still alive. It was a shame that Taliban attack had put him permanently on the disabled list. The nation had lost something that day.

Having him here brought back a whole flood of memories—about being younger, about still having a husband, about still having an exciting career. Fixing the tea in my perfect little kitchen looking out at my lovely little garden, I felt like I had left the best years behind me.

Oh, I know I shouldn't feel sorry for myself. I have a wonderful family, some nice friends, and a good pension. I had a lot more than most people, and yet I couldn't help but feel a bit useless. The world had kept on moving, and here I was in Cheerville.

*Buck up, Barbara,* I told myself. *The world has indeed kept on moving, and it's bringing you along with it. There's a CIA agent in your living room, and he's obviously not here to sample your tea. Time to get useful.*

I squared my shoulders as much as my sore back would permit and went out to the living room. These little episodes of self-pity had started when James had passed and welled up more and more frequently as the years crept on. I had faced many frightening things in my life and had defeated most of them. I suppose I feared death and aging so much because they were undefeatable.

*Stop. You have a mission to do.*

"So, what's next?" I asked as I set the tray down.

Gary laughed. "You haven't changed a bit."

"Oh, I don't know about that," I said as I eased myself into my chair.

He shifted in his seat. "Things have... accelerated. We thought at first that this was a simple revenge killing with a raised middle finger to the CIA in the form of dumping the victim into your shopping cart. Now it looks like a lot more is going on."

I poured him some tea. "So do I actually get to be filled in now?"

Gary sighed. "You do. To a point. You know how the agency works."

"Need-to-know basis. I'm surprised they didn't make us tattoo the words on our forehead. Well, go on."

Gary gently removed Dandelion from his pants leg, where she was busy fraying the fabric of his slacks.

"It all goes back to when we were agents down there, when General Noriega was in power. We and other teams were busy trying to take down the drug barons to remove his financial base."

"That didn't work too well," I said. It's hard to arrest criminals when the government is complicit. Even those we got rid of in more, ahem, *direct* ways, only ended up getting replaced that same week.

"Nor did the coups we arranged."

We had arranged three different coup attempts led by various disaffected officers in the police and military. You can read all about them in some good history books published since the war. Well, two of them. The third coup attempt was crushed so quickly it never even made the news.

And that's the one Gary started talking about.

"After our first two coup attempts failed, Noriega was getting paranoid and was watching his forces like a hawk. We had a hard time organizing a third, remember? But we thought we had a good one."

"I remember."

The leader, Carlos Pretto, was the head of a rural police district that had been left impoverished by the regime. The narcos ran the area and had brought a lot of ill will onto themselves by killing off anyone they didn't like. Pretto was unusual among the police commanders in that he wasn't corrupt. He tried to do his job, but with the current regime he could barely keep his job, let alone do it. And he had survived at least one assassination attempt by the narcos.

People feared the narcos but also hated them. If the police could throw off Noriega's corruption and take a stand against the drug barons, the people might rise up. Commander Pretto also had allies in several other district stations and among the military. If he showed the nation that his police district wasn't corrupt and got rid of the local drug barons, he could create a power base that would have a ripple effect in the other districts. Noriega would be faced with a revolt in the countryside and international embarrassment for having his drug connections proven once and for all, and he'd have his main money supply dry up. The rebels, on the other hand, would get U.S. government funding plus all the weapons they could take from local armories and from the drug militias, which were considerable. Noriega would be overthrown.

At least, that was the theory.

The reality didn't work out so well.

Commander Pretto had been careful. In the middle of the night, he personally led a group of trusted officers into the police barracks and arrested everyone he suspected of being a Noriega spy. Then he had taken his men and swooped down on the local drug baron's ranch.

They moved in, guns blazing, taking the drug baron's hacienda and the drug baron himself and securing the cocaine-processing lab and a storehouse full of cocaine ready for the marketplace.

What they didn't know was that an army patrol was coming to pick up the cocaine that very night. Just as his lightly armed police officers were celebrating an easy victory, several armored cars armed with machine guns drove onto the ranch. A fierce gunfight ensued with Pretto and his men holed up in the hacienda and the soldiers picking them off. The troops radioed for backup in the form of a couple of tanks. When Pretto saw these behemoths rumbling up the driveway, they surrendered. Pretto and his officers were summarily executed, and his men were thrown into prison, as were Pretto's and the officers' families. They were later saved by the U.S. troops during the invasion.

The whole thing had been hushed up. Noriega didn't want to tell the press, which he tightly controlled, because it put him on the side of the narcos. The U.S. didn't want to talk about it because it had been such an abysmal failure and they would have had to admit they were trying to overthrow Noriega.

"When we released the coup leaders' families from that stinking hole they had been locked in, we offered them visas," Gary said. "Sort of an apology. Most took them. Noriega had confiscated all of their property, and while they got their homes and land back, all other portable wealth was gone. Commander Pretto had come from one of the region's leading families, which was probably why he had been able to keep his job despite pressure from Noriega and the narcos. His father had owned some mines, and one of his discoveries was the Volcano Stone of Panama. That got confiscated along with the rest of the family's wealth."

"Oh dear. And the president of Escudo Security is... "

"Ricardo Pretto, the police commander's son, now going under the name of Ricardo Morales. He is the oldest surviving member of the family and is the rightful heir of all that stolen property. Everyone in the company is related to one of the coup officers.

We've known about them for years, and they've kept quiet until now."

"Until Sir Edmund bought the Volcano Stone of Panama."

Gary nodded, his mouth set in a grim line. "Montalbion didn't know it had been stolen. The Noriega regime had faked a legal bill of sale signed by old man Pretto at gunpoint and sold it to an international dealer. From there, it passed through several private hands before being bought quite publicly by Montalbion."

"That must have seemed like a godsend to the folks at Escudo Security."

"Indeed. And instead of trying to fight a long legal battle with someone who could afford top lawyers, they decided to take what they felt was truly theirs."

"That doesn't forgive murder."

"No. They've gone way out of line. We need to reel them in. What have you found out since we talked last?"

I told him everything I had learned so far, finishing with the planting of the GPS device on the car just an hour before.

He smiled at that and took a sip of tea. "You do

know it's illegal to plant a location device on someone without their written consent?"

"Cell phones are location devices. No one kicks up a fuss about that."

"People give their consent. It's in that long user agreement no one reads."

"Because it's written in Sumerian. You have to have degrees in law and engineering to understand those things. I suppose it's the same with those virtual assistants that listen in on your conversations."

Gary chuckled. "Oh yes, people actually pay to have their homes bugged. That's something I would have never predicted back in the Cold War."

"So am I in trouble for acting in an illegal fashion toward the poor, innocent folks of Escudo Security?"

Gary waved a dismissive hand. "This is the CIA, not the Girl Scouts. It's not like we're bringing them to trial anyway."

I put my teacup down. "We're not?"

"No. This has to be done quietly."

"So when do the field agents come?"

Gary winced. "They don't."

"What? No field agents?"

"No."

"They're leaving this to a retired agent and an agent on desk duty."

"Things are really busy right now with the terrorist threat turned up. The Panamanians are low priority."

I studied him. "Come on, Junior. I wasn't born yesterday, as my back keeps reminding me. Does the agency know you're here?"

He looked away. "I took a couple of personal days."

I groaned. I knew something was off about this.

"So what's really going on?"

Gary wouldn't look at me.

After a long moment, he spoke.

"We messed up," he said. "And I don't mean the Agency but the three of us. Remember that little beachside restaurant in La Palma, where we met with some of the family members after they were released?"

I nodded. It had been a beautiful place, looking out at the sea. Golden sands, crystal-clear waters, and me, James, and Gary all hyped up and keeping watch for an ambush. The invasion had happened just a month before, and while some Panamanians loved us, others didn't. The bombing had been messy in places and, as usual, innocent people had gotten caught in the crossfire.

We had met with the heads of households of some of the families that had been involved in the Commander Pretto coup. We explained how we promised them visas, protection, and that we would trace any stolen property. Then we had handed them over to another set of agents to take care of them. Our job was done, and we were off to the next country and the next assignment.

I never saw those people again, and I had assumed the CIA had kept all its promises. Apparently, it had not.

"So you're saying they're angry because we didn't get them all their property back? Fair enough, but that doesn't excuse murder."

"It's worse than that. Much worse. That second CIA team had different orders than ours and didn't bother to fill us in."

"Need-to-know basis again?"

He nodded sadly. "Yeah. I only pieced it together over the years, and only now have I been in a position to help. The Agency decided that they were only going to give visas to the coup members' direct families, not the extended families like they promised.

And to cover their tracks, instead of giving them a direct flight to the United States and a new identity, they made them stay in Mexico for five years. I suppose that was to cover their tracks, deny any involvement in Pretto's attempted coup. They gave them barely enough to live on. Five years of misery and uncertainty after a spell in Noriega's dungeon."

"And they had to leave their extended families behind," I said. "All the old people and the cousins and aunts and uncles. Oh Junior, you know how families are in Latin America. They don't distinguish between nuclear and extended family! And with all their portable property gone, they must have been impoverished."

"Yeah, the Agency stabbed them in the back. They did get U.S. visas five years later, but the bitterness must have already set in."

"That still doesn't excuse murder," I insisted. "What are we going to do about this?"

He raised his hands. "I have no idea."

"But why isn't the Agency trying to make good?"

"They want to let the past remain in the past. I can't."

"No," I said and sighed. "I can't either."

I checked the GPS tracker.

"Well, whatever we do, we need to do it now," I said.

"Why?"

"Because that car I put a trace on is heading out of town."

Gary and I took his car, a late-model sports car that was obviously evidence of a middle-aged man harkening back to his youth. I didn't rib him about it. He had a heck of a youth, and he was justified in wanting to relive it.

I was getting to relive mine too. As we sped along the main route through town in pursuit of the Escudo Security car, I felt more alive than I had in years.

I had Junior at my side, we were both checking our pistols, and we were tracking a target vehicle. I felt great.

Until the target vehicle moved out of range and disappeared from my GPS locator.

## TWELVE

"It's gone! They must have gotten onto the highway and sped up," I said.

Just then we got stuck at a red light.

"Ugh! They're probably going to the burial site to retrieve the stone and move it like they said they would. I can't imagine why else they would be going out of town in that direction. There's only country-side this way."

"Hold on."

Gary glanced either way to make sure no cars were coming and slammed on the gas.

We ran through the intersection and shot through downtown, past the old Colonial church and town commons, and blew a stop sign at the far side.

"Junior, I do believe you're enjoying this."

He let out a laugh. "Better than driving a desk in Langley."

A siren wailed behind us. Red and blue lights flashed in our rearview mirror.

"What a time for the Cheerville police to be doing their job!" I cried.

"Has the car appeared on the trace?"

"No. We have to catch up to them."

"How good are the local police?"

A loud cackle was the only answer I could manage.

It told Gary all he needed to know. He hit the gas again and took off down a narrow road past tidy little homes. The police car picked up speed too.

"Watch this," Gary said. A side street was coming up, way too fast. He'd never be able to make that turn.

He knew it, too, so he cut across the lawn of the house on the corner, tearing up the grass and obliterating a garden gnome.

"Always hated those things," he muttered, the car jolting as it got back on the pavement and he shot off down the new street.

I glanced in the rearview mirror. The policeman

had decided not to risk the wrath of all gnomekind and had slammed on his brakes, screeching to a halt just past the intersection.

"He'll back up and be on us in a moment," I said.

"No problem."

He zigzagged through a residential neighborhood, swerving to avoid cars, taking out a couple of mailboxes, and generally causing havoc. The police siren faded behind us.

"I must say, Junior, your driving is quite good. Have you been practicing?"

"I was a crack driver back in the day too. Don't you remember how I used to drive a Jeep?"

"No."

"Oh. Well, I was good."

"If you say so. I don't recall you killing any gnomes in Panama or Syria."

"I don't think they have them over there."

"Maybe if they did, they'd have more stable governments."

We got on the highway. Still no sign of the car on my GPS locator.

"Where could they be?" I grumbled.

"There's an off-ramp coming up. The sign says it leads to a county road. Should we try that?"

I looked over the countryside, a patchwork of woods and fields and the occasional large home.

"I think they went further out. Keep driving."

My phone rang. Albert.

"This isn't exactly the best time," I said, glancing at my GPS locator and still seeing nothing.

"I figured out how the murderer managed to dump the body on you and get away without you spotting him."

"Have you now?"

The doubt in my voice must have been obvious because he said defensively, "I'm not lit. I'm, like, totally sober. Okay, maybe still a bit buzzed from last night, but—"

Big sigh. "Albert, could you please get to the point?"

"Look, you know how Ms. Nightingale found a bar-code sticker on the catwalk and the pigs found one for the same product in the shopping cart?"

"Don't call them pigs. They're police officers."

Gary gave me a questioning look. I waved him off.

"Whatever. The stickers prove the drones did it."

"You're high. I'm hanging up now."

"No, listen! The bar-code stickers are always on

the top of the packaging. The drones sense them and then stack the boxes on top of each other. The drone saw the label on the dead dude, saw the label on the shopping cart, and tried to stack the dead dude in the shopping cart."

"Oh, come on."

"It totally explains everything!"

"No, it doesn't. Let me walk you through this. I'll speak slowly so my words get through the fog. The drones aren't intelligent. They're not going to wait for me to pass by before stacking Sir Edmund onto my shopping cart. They can't lift him anyway. The drones can only carry up to 30 pounds."

"That's just the safety limit. They can actually carry, like, 50, but it's hard on their engines."

"So a drone still couldn't lift him."

"Two drones could. They're programmed to work together."

"But how would they know to wait for me to show up? Why not just fly over to the row of shopping carts and drop him there?" The image of Sir Edmund Montalbion flying across the upper reaches of SerMart with a knife through his head flashed through my mind's eye. That would have been interesting to see in real life.

"They must have got hacked, same as the camera system."

"Oh." Well, that made sense, didn't it? I was impressed. We had explained the whole situation to Albert and everything we knew about the case, but I hadn't thought that he would actually remember a tenth of it. "So those men from the security company who came last night must have been searching for the tag. They realized it could be a vital clue, and when one of their drones spotted it on the catwalk, they decided to come and retrieve it."

"Yeah. They were dumb to do that in the first place, but when they saw the tag had come off the body and stuck to the catwalk, they decided to get it. They couldn't get the drones to grab it because they only have grabbers on the bottom. The drones couldn't have pulled it off the edge of the catwalk."

"I must say, Albert, you can be quite intelligent when you want to be. If you stopped smoking, you could go places."

"That's what Octavian says. He's, like, a motivational speaker or something."

"Perhaps you should listen to him more, and perhaps you should stop lying to him about having quit smoking."

There was silence on the other end of the line.

"Yeah," he said at last. "Yeah, he's a good dude."

I said goodbye and hung up.

"Who was that?" Gary asked.

"A young stoner who's been helping out with the case. My boyfriend seems to have inherited him."

He gave me a curious glance. "Inherited from who?"

"Parents who didn't do their job."

"Sounds like you're having an interesting retirement."

"You might say that. Hey! There they are!"

A red dot had appeared just on the upper right edge of my sensor. They were a good ten miles off, and judging from the location they were already off the highway.

Gary picked up speed, passing by commuter cars and the occasional truck. There was a tense moment as a state highway patrol passed going the other direction on the divided highway, but the trooper didn't turn around.

The dot kept moving for a few minutes, but much more slowly than we did. I guessed they were on a rural road, maybe an unpaved one. The distance between us narrowed.

After a couple more miles and times checking

the map, I said, "I think this next off-ramp is the right one."

A police siren wailed in the distance. Far behind, we could see the flash of lights weaving through traffic. Gary got a car between us and them and got down the off-ramp as fast as he could.

"Did we shake them?" he asked.

I checked the rearview mirror. "Not sure. I don't see anything. They might be trying to cut us off on the access road."

We got past the access road and onto a narrow county road without seeing our pursuers and breathed a little easier.

But not for long, because now we were closing in on that baleful red dot we had been chasing. It wasn't moving anymore.

Trees closed in on either side, broken by the occasional field or pond. There were no houses in sight. Gary slowed, peering to the left and right. He put his gun on the dashboard.

"Good place for an ambush," he muttered.

Oh dear. He was right. I pulled my 9mm out of my purse and held onto it. I slouched down a bit in the seat to make a smaller target, but that sent a twinge along my spine, so I had to sit back up properly. All those lectures about the importance of posture I had given Martin, and Frederick when he was a boy, came back to me. What goes around comes around.

The car we were tracking was a mile ahead and a bit to the left. We found a rutted old dirt road bypassing a dilapidated and obviously abandoned farm. The road ran off into the woods.

"They're down there," he said, slowing to a stop. "We should probably walk so they don't hear us."

I checked the sensor. Still nearly a mile. I thought about my back and Gary's leg and said, "Let's take it slow and go another half mile. They won't hear us, and we'll be closer to the car if we have to make an escape."

Gary only nodded. He had probably been thinking of his knee and my back too. Driving closer was risky, but us ending up more disabled than we already were before we even got to the scene might prove even riskier.

The path got more rutted as we continued, Gary's car trundling along and splashing through some puddles. We could see several fresh tracks. At least a couple of vehicles. I didn't dare get out and take a closer look. Instead I darted glances at the trees to either side, expecting an ambush at any second.

"At least we'll block their way out of here," Gary whispered.

That was true. The road didn't widen at any spot, so they wouldn't be able to get around us.

That also meant we wouldn't be able to turn around.

After half a mile, Gary parked and cut the engine. Taking a deep breath, we both took the safeties off our guns and got out. I put on my reading glasses. Gary gave me a curious look but said nothing.

He took the left side of the road and I took the right, getting into the underbrush and moving along a few yards in from the road. Luckily, the forest was thin. Probably a century ago, it had been farmland that had been abandoned and later reclaimed by nature.

Even so, it was slow going for the both of us. I remembered a time when he and I and my late husband, James, had to sprint down the tarmac of a rural air base to catch a military transport plane that was just taking off. We were late because of some trouble with the local militia, and the pilot had received orders to leave. Just as he taxied down the runway, we appeared behind him.

There was no chance for the pilot to stop, so we

had no choice but to run with our sixty-pound packs after him. The copilot got to the back and opened the door for us, waving us on.

We all made it. Barely, but we made it. I jumped in first, then Junior leapt in and landed right on top of me, and then just as the plane lost contact with the ground, James vaulted in, landing on both of us. As the plane flew into the air, taking fire from enemies on the ground, we all lay in a cackling sweaty heap, joking about our narrow escape.

Ah, those were the days!

And now they were back, albeit in a slower, more arthritic form.

I saw a clearing up ahead. I peeked through the underbrush, caught Gary's attention, and signaled that we should withdraw.

Once we got a hundred yards back, he crossed the road and joined me. Then we moved ahead together.

Soon the clearing came into view. We peered through the trees and bushes, trying to make out details without getting too close.

The clearing was the remnant of another old farm. The farmhouse had collapsed to its foundations, but the yard was on rocky ground and still reasonably clear of undergrowth. The car we had been following was parked next to the four-by-four. Several men stood near the ruined old house. I recognized Ricardo Morales, really Ricardo Pretto, president of Escudo Security and son of the man who had died trying to help the United States and his own nation.

Around him stood four younger men and a man who must have been in his eighties. They were all looking at something in a small tin box that Ricardo was holding.

I motioned to Gary that we should move forward, but slowly. I wanted to see what was in that box. It had me curious, because they looked like they weren't looking at a gemstone. They all had their heads cocked in the same direction, and Ricardo was holding the box out so they could all see clearly inside. It was like they were reading or looking at a picture.

We crept forward, taking each step with care and watching where we placed our feet. One step. Another. I glanced up. Was that the corner of a piece of paper sticking out of the box? Another step. Another.

I don't know what I did, whether I turned in an odd way or I tensed up too much or my muscles finally decided to call it a day, but a lance of pain jabbed me in the lower back.

I managed not to cry out, but I did stagger to the side, and before I could right myself, I had rustled the bush next to me.

The men turned, drawing guns from their pockets or shoulder holsters.

# THIRTEEN

The first shot clipped a small branch above me, making it drop right on my head. The second bullet whickered through the nearby underbrush, clipping leaves as it passed.

I dropped to the ground, ignoring the protest in my back. A bullet through the gut would be a lot more painful.

All five of the Panamanians had drawn pistols and spread out to take cover. Ricardo, the old man, and one of the young men got behind the engine block of the four-by-four. Another ducked behind the remains of a brick chimney. The other two dove behind the wall of the house.

And all five of them blasted away at us like nobody's business.

I adjusted my glasses, aimed at both vehicles, and took out a tire on each of them. Gary busied himself by chipping away at the brick chimney.

That got them to put their heads down for a second. We used the opportunity to shift position a few yards to the right. Remarkably, my back didn't lock up. That would have been seriously bad news.

Then they opened up again. From the direction of their shots, I could tell they weren't sure exactly where we were. They searched for us with their bullets, and once or twice they nearly found us.

The two who had disappeared behind the house didn't fire. That worried me.

"I think the rear two are circling around to flank us," Gary said.

"You took the words right out of my mouth."

"Let's head them off."

"Wait a second." I raised my voice. "Ricardo Pretto! The police are on their way. They know who you are, and they know you and your men killed Sir Edmund for the Volcano Stone. Give yourself up and the CIA can help."

All that got me was another fusillade, this time closer. They had sensed the location of my voice pretty well. These guys had obviously had some training, probably from one of the older exiles. Most had been in the police or military.

"I tried," I muttered. "Let's go."

We fired a few more times, smashing the windows of the four-by-four and perforating the side, then crawled back a bit, Gary wincing from his knee wound and me wincing from my back. The two of us were in a real fix. Once we put a few more yards between us and them, we got up and moved to the right, hoping to head off whoever was coming at us from that direction.

We didn't have long to wait. The guy had moved fast, or at least fast from the point of view of someone who by all rights should be at home quietly drinking tea and petting her kitten.

He came creeping up a dry creek bed that gave him some cover.

Unfortunately for him, it was the obvious route, and Gary and I were waiting on opposite sides of the opening. When he came out, he got a quick warning and two guns pointed at his head.

I was right. They had been trained well. Most people would either freeze or immediately fire in that situation. If he froze, he'd get all of one second to drop his gun or I'd be forced to shoot to protect myself and my old partner. If he fired, we'd have to kill him.

Luckily, he did the smart thing. He might have gotten one of us but not both of us. Not at the angles we were at.

He dropped his gun and raised his hands.

His fear was quickly replaced by annoyance when he saw a grandmother wearing a pair of reading glasses and a limping middle-aged man come out of the bushes.

"Guns are guns no matter who wields them," I said by way of reassurance. I said it in Spanish, trying to lay on a Panamanian accent.

He frowned at me, stepping away from his gun without having to be asked.

When Gary bent to pick it up, the Panamanian kicked a small stone into the side of his head. He followed this with a kick to the head then a karate chop to my hand that made my gun go flying.

He had done it all so fast I hadn't had time to react.

At least he had been gentlemanly enough not to hit me hard. With his level of skill, he could have broken my wrist. Instead, he put just enough force into it to make me drop my pistol.

In a flash, he grabbed both guns and held them on us.

"Dad! Grandpa! I got them."

"Grandpa?" Gary asked, trying to get to his feet.

"You don't know half of what you think you know, gringo."

As the young man said this, he turned a bit away from me, giving me a chance to retrieve my pepper spray. When he turned back to me, he got a full dose in the face.

Pro tip: never underestimate your enemy, even if your enemy is a sweet little old lady.

*Especially* if your enemy is a sweet little old lady.

He staggered, choking and coughing, guns firing, the bullets whizzing to either side of me as I did an unhappy dance.

Then Gary laid him out with a bit of karate of his own.

The young man was probably better at hand-to-hand combat than Gary was at this stage in his life, but it's hard to fight when your eyes feel like two eggs frying in a hot pan.

Gary scooped up the pistols and handed one back to me just in time for us to hear the sound of running feet coming in our direction.

I aimed my gun at the moaning form on the ground.

"It's over."

Ricardo was in front. Our eyes locked. I held my gun steady, aimed right at the young man I took to be his son. I saw the calculations go on behind Ricardo's eyes.

Would I shoot? If I hesitated, he could kill me. But then Gary would fire and at least one of them would die before Gary went down too.

But if I didn't hesitate, if I carried through my threat...

Ricardo cursed in Spanish and tossed his gun to the ground. The others, one by one, slowly did the same.

"Thank you," I said after taking a deep breath. "I didn't want to do that."

"Would you have?" Ricardo asked, helping his son up.

I didn't reply. I wasn't sure myself.

We herded the Panamanians back to the cars, keeping well behind them and covering them with our guns. The old man stood by the car, a weary look on his face. He was unarmed. I noticed a livid old scar across his neck.

And suddenly it all became clear.

"Police Commander Carlos Pretto, I presume?"

He nodded. In a gravelly voice he said, "No one has called me that in many, many years."

"I thought you died."

"So did Noriega. They decided not to kill me by firing squad. They said that was too honorable for a traitor, so they cut my throat and dumped me in a field. Like an animal. Like a dog. Luckily a farmer found me and nursed me back to health."

I glanced at Gary. He looked just as surprised as I was.

The young man I pepper sprayed was still moaning. I allowed Ricardo to fetch some water from the four-by-four to rinse his eyes.

"Why didn't you tell the CIA? You could have gotten a visa," Gary said.

Carlos Pretto spat. "Spend five years in Mexico living like a peasant, hoping to finally come to the country that cheated my family? No. I got a new identity, a Panamanian one, and then I went hunting for all the things Noriega stole from us. I have found some, and a few days ago I came here on a tourist visa and found another."

"Why did you have him killed? Sir Edmund was an innocent man!"

"No one who buys stolen property is an innocent man."

"He didn't know it was stolen."

"Yes, he did. We told him. He made his excuses, talking about the bill of sale my father made to General Noriega, all this nonsense. He knew it was all a lie, but he saw a pretty stone and he wanted it."

"That doesn't forgive murder."

His eyes glinted. "I was a forgiving man once. I am no longer."

"But why put him in SerMart? And why dump him on me?"

"He was a proud man. He deserved to be dumped in the place he hated. As for you, I wanted to send a message. It was only the first part of the message."

"And the rest?" I asked.

"The rest is here," Gary said. He had retrieved the tin box they had been looking at before the gunfight. Gary leafed through the papers and photos within.

"The Volcano Stone of Panama for one. But also documents, photos, signed affidavits. All the proof you need to show the CIA tried a third coup attempt," Gary looked over at our captives, "and then let down the ones who risked their lives for us."

"What were you going to do with this?" I asked.

"Sell it to the press. Shame the United States into doing the right thing for us. But you caught us, and now I am going to prison for murder."

"You?" Gary said. "You don't have the strength to drive a knife through someone's head. You must be what? Eighty?"

"I did it, and I will tell the court so."

I looked carefully around at the younger men, all with their hands up. All except for the youngest member of the Pretto clan, who was still having his eyes washed out with water. Was that a faint bruise I saw on his cheek?

I looked back at Carlos Pretto, who glanced nervously from his grandson to me.

Our eyes locked.

"I have died once for my country and my family. Let me do so again."

I nodded.

Gary held up the papers. "I cannot let these be seen."

"Go ahead and take them," the old police chief said in his raspy voice. "It does not matter. We have copies in the hands of a trusted friend you will never find. Copies are not as convincing as originals, that is true, but they will still embarrass the United States."

"Embarrassing us won't help you," I said. "What if Gary and I lean on the CIA to help you recover your property, or at least pay compensation? I cannot let a murder charge pass, but the rest of you I could get off without having to go to jail. As for you, Commander Pretto, I could at least keep you from facing the death penalty."

He waved a dismissive hand. "I am eighty-two years old and have lung cancer. Death and I have been companions for some time now. Do what you can for my family, and I will not release the documents."

"We need some reassurances," Gary said.

Carlos Pretto looked at him. "You have my word of honor."

I nodded. "That's good enough."

"Hold it right there!"

We all turned. Arnold Grimal emerged from the woods, a pair of policemen flanking him. All had guns drawn.

"What's going on here?" he demanded.

Gary flashed a badge. "That's classified."

Grimal turned the color of a tomato. "Classified? You careen through town, have a gun battle in the forest, and tear up my front lawn, and you're telling me it's classified?"

I giggled. "That was your lawn we drove across?"

"Yes, it was!"

"And your garden gnome?"

"What's that got to do with anything!" Grimal barked.

Gary and I burst out with laughter.

After we got a hold of ourselves, we told the police what they needed to hear, and let them lead away old Carlos Pretto. The rest got to go, although that took a great deal of convincing on our part. As I argued with Grimal, I saw Gary sidle up to Ricardo and slip something into his pocket, something small and round that flashed like fire. I gave him a wink.

At last we finished, and we headed back to our car. The Panamanian vehicles were wrecked. We made them walk. They should have to pay at least a little bit for all the trouble they caused.

Gary walked with the tin box under his arm.

"That was a good deed you did, Junior."

He nodded. "Working the desk for so long, I forgot how complicated all this stuff can get, how you have to compromise some of your ethics for the greater good."

"And it does get messy. The Panamanians were right. At least we have balanced that out a little today."

"We'll balance it out more," Gary said. "You and I will get to work tomorrow pulling on the right strings. The Pretto family and all the other families deserve the compensation they were promised all those years go."

"And I deserve a long hot bath. I better check in with Octavian. I said I'd call him. Let's see if I can get a signal out here."

I checked my phone, and then stared at the time and date in shock.

"Oh my God, I almost forgot!" I cried.

## FOURTEEN

Gary stared at me, worry etched on his face. "What?"

"I can't believe this," I moaned. "I've been so careful, planned everything so well, and then I mess it all up at the last minute."

"What happened? Did someone get away? Was the Volcano Stone switched with a replica? Tell me!"

"I forgot my grandson's birthday party. It's on right now!"

"A birthday party?"

"Yes! I'm going to be late! Oh, what an idiot I've been."

"We just survived a gunfight, and you're worried about a kid's birthday party."

"Come on. Drive me back to my house. I need to

get his gift. Never mind the red lights, I'll handle the chief of police!"

After a frantic race across town, me rushing in and grabbing his present, and then another frantic race to the skate park, we made it just in time.

The indoor skate park was a converted warehouse on the edge of town that had been filled with ramps and humps of concrete so young people who thought they were invincible could fly around on skateboards doing unlikely tricks and making spectacular crashes. The interior walls were all covered in graffiti (encouraged by the city council because it reduced the amount of graffiti elsewhere), and to one side was a burger bar. That's where the party was being held.

We headed for it on a walkway around the outer edge of the skate park, protected from the skaters by one of those clear barriers they use in hockey rinks.

A good thing, too, because a teenager slammed into the barrier right next to us at a high enough velocity that his beanie flew off.

"Ouch," I said.

"Oh, he'll be fine," Gary replied. Indeed, the boy was up, beanie and all, and shooting for a ramp before you could say "hairline fracture."

All over the skate park, which was the size of a

football field, teen boys and a few girls were zipping around on their boards, doing the most amazing things. It really was impressive to see, almost beautiful.

One girl of about twelve who caught my eye stood at the top of a steep ramp twice as tall as she was. She stood balanced on her board, only the back part of it on the lip of the precipice, the rest hanging over. With a snap, she brought it down and in the blink of an eye shot down the ramp, sped along an open part, hit another low ramp and flew into the air. Her board spun beneath her, and I thought I was going to see another bad crash, but it landed upright and she landed on it. She banked around another ramp and zoomed back the way she had come. It took me a second to realize that flipping her board in midair had been part of the trick.

"They should make agents do this in field training to learn balance and dexterity," Gary said.

"And fearlessness," I added. "Keep mum, Junior. I've never told any of my family what I used to be."

"Smart move, mum. Mum's the word."

As we got to the burger bar, Martin waved from amid a crowd of his friends.

"Hey, Grandma!"

I felt a flush of pride and acceptance. Here he

was, surrounded by other teenagers, and he acknowl-
edged my existence! The carefully wrapped present
in my hands probably didn't hurt.

He got up and limped over, a fresh scrape on one
knee.

"What happened?" I asked.

"He totally wiped out trying to grind the bowl!"
one of his friends said. "It was epic!"

I had no idea what that young man had just said,
but apparently Martin wiping out and drawing blood
was a good thing, something to win approval.
Bleeding got more points with your peers than an A-
plus in English. Way more.

"You're just in time," Martin said, his gaze
straying to a pile of packages on the table.

"Well then, maybe I'll have the honor of having
my present opened first."

"Sure!" He turned uncertainly to Gary.
"Um, hi."

"Oh, how silly of me. This is my friend, Gary
Wycliff. He was in town, and I wanted to see him. I
haven't seen him in so long. I hope you don't mind
him coming."

"No problem. The cake is huge. Pleased to meet
you." Martin and Gary shook hands. I felt glad to see

Martin on his best behavior today, with the exception of bloodying himself.

"Here you go," I said, handing over the present.

"Cool!"

Everyone gathered around as Martin sat down and started tearing at the paper. My son and daughter-in-law smiled at me from the other side of a sea of adolescent heads, all bent over to see what he got.

"Awesome! A FriendZip Bracelet Fun Pak!"

"Oh, hey!" The boy who had told me of Martin's accident shouted. "Now I can give you a skateboard token."

It was only then that I noticed he wore a FriendZip Bracelet on his slim wrist.

"We'll trade a football one," another boy said, pulling his own FriendZip Bracelet off his wrist and unzipping it.

Soon a bunch of his friends were trading tokens like Wall Street stockbrokers trading blue chip shares.

I basked in the glow of coolness. I had bridged two generations and picked the right gift.

"Hey, what's this gunk?" Martin said. He had noticed one end of the box was crumpled. Some dried material was stuck on the corner, a deep red.

I nearly keeled over right there. Florence

Nightingale had given me the very same box that got crushed by Sir Edmund. There was blood on my grandson's birthday present.

"Looks like raspberry jam," one of his friends said.

"Don't touch that," I said quickly. "It's, um, makeup. I spilled some or... something. Better wash your hands before you eat."

"Doesn't look like makeup," one of the girls said.

"It is. Um, for old ladies. You'll know all about it one day, honey."

"Uh, okay," Martin said with a shrug. To my relief, he didn't touch the bloodstain. Once he emptied the box and was distracted trading tokens with his friends, I surreptitiously grabbed the box and threw it in the nearest trash can. Only Gary noticed. He gave me a wink. I hadn't told him about the present being crushed, but he knew a bloodstain when he saw one.

After the token trading was over, Martin opened his other presents. He got a new soccer ball, a couple of jerseys he had asked for, some new parts for his skateboard (why the metal bits that hold the wheels are called "trucks" remains a mystery to me), and the hottest new video game. It was called Jungle Combat ("The Most Realistic

Fighting Game Ever!"). Gary and I suppressed a snicker.

Once the feeding frenzy was over and Martin was sitting content in a heap of destroyed wrapping paper, he held up his FriendZip Bracelet and rattled it.

"Thanks, Grandma. This is the best."

Gary stepped forward. "Well, young man. While I don't know you, I don't think it would be fair for me to eat some of your cake without giving you something. You might have noticed that I limp. I used to be in the... army. When I was younger, I fought the Taliban. That was right at the beginning of the war, before you were even born." His face got a faraway look for a moment. "Yes, it's been going on a long time. I got wounded in the leg there. An RPG hit the Hummer I was in and ripped open the side. Ripped open my leg too."

The kids had gone completely silent. Everyone was giving him their rapt attention. Gary went on.

"That was the end of the war for me. Now I work a desk job for the government. To remember those times, I wear this." He pulled a leather thong that was hidden beneath his shirt and brought out a jagged bit of metal encased in clear plastic resin. "This is part of the shrapnel they took out of me. I wear it for luck. Now I'm not going to give you this, it's a bit too personal. I'm sure you understand. But I do want to give you this."

He reached into his pocket and brought out a spent cartridge.

"This is a spent bullet cartridge from a Taliban AK-47. I gathered this after one of the firefights I was in."

Martin gaped. He gingerly reached out and took it.

"Whoa. Thanks, mister."

His friends gathered around.

"Awesome!"

"Incredible!"

"That's totally epic!"

Martin smiled at Gary. "Thanks, man. This is the best present I ever got. I'll keep this forever."

I put my hands on my hips. I go through gunfights and murders to get him the coolest teen collectible on the market and get upstaged by an old friend who has never even met my grandson before?

Humph!

# ABOUT THE AUTHOR

Harper Lin is a *USA TODAY* bestselling cozy mystery author. When she's not reading or writing mysteries, she loves going to yoga classes, hiking, and hanging out with her family and friends.

For a complete list of her books by series, visit her website.

www.HarperLin.com